TRUTH WE BEAR

A PIECES OF ME NOVEL
BOOK TWO

DANIELLE ROSE

TRUTH WE BEAR

A PIECES OF ME NOVEL
BOOK TWO

DANIELLE ROSE

WATERHOUSE PRESS

For P.—

For showing me true love knows no bounds.

CHAPTER ONE

The wind shifted, and the threads from an old weeping willow tree caught my eye. Weepers, as I liked to call them, were my favorite trees. I could swing from their vine-like branches as if I were Tarzan in search of Jane. I could hide behind its thick base during a game of tag. Too often Mother would find me napping beneath its shade.

Again, the breeze shifted, sending the aroma of the sweetest wildflowers to my nose. I inhaled deeply, long, slow breaths. I'd considered snagging a few from the outskirts of the field for Mother. She always liked it when Father brought her flowers. I liked the way her nose crinkled when she smiled. The scent of flowers made me do that too.

When spring came, we often had class outside, in God's land. I loved being outdoors—and not only because the schoolhouse had too few windows to allow the breeze to dry my sweat. I felt free when I was outside. I felt like I was part of God's plan. But when I was within the log-cabin walls of the schoolhouse, even though Father had helped build it with his own hands, I felt cut off from the world, from God.

Smack!

"James!" the teacher yelled. "I will not tell you to pay attention again." A crater marked the earth where she had whipped it with her stick.

"I'm sorry, ma'am," I said in my most grown-up voice. Mother had always told me to respect and trust my elders. After all, it was our core belief system at Living Light. And I did so wholeheartedly.

"James, repeat the Creed."

I nodded and regurgitated the list of rules I had sworn to follow as a member of Living Light. "I shall always obey my elders."

The schoolteacher nodded, and I continued.

"What I do, I do for God."

"And the last?" she asked.

"I shall forsake all others outside of Living Light."

"Well done."

I was born here, but my parents weren't. Tired of the day-to-day life in corporate America, they fled, bought this land, and started anew, creating a self-sufficient community today's hippies would envy. Soon after, their friends, who also desired to leave the modern world behind, joined us. By word of mouth, and only to the most deserving, our little community grew tenfold. Together, we cared for each other, bringing our knowledge of the other world to Living Light.

The schoolteacher used to teach in the other world, but I'd overheard her say how much she hated it. She was new here. She came after the new pastor joined. I missed my old teacher. She was nice, and she never hit us. She worked in laundry now. Our new teacher told us fear was God's greatest motivator, and she would instill that fear within us and to our very core.

Sometimes, in hushed tones, Mother and Father spoke about the other world. I think they missed it—or maybe they just missed how Living Light used to be. After the new pastor joined, everything started to change.

Our gardener used to box our excess food and sell it at a stand near the city. He always returned empty-handed but pockets full. But now, commingling with the outside folk was forbidden.

No outside-world contact at all, my new teacher would say. No television, no computers, no access to the outside world... I didn't know what a television or computer was, but the moment she told me I couldn't have it, I desperately wanted one. I wondered if my parents and the other leaders felt that way too.

I didn't think Mother and Father were happy anymore, but they wouldn't abandon all they'd created. They were loyal to Living Light and their community. I hoped I'd inherited that same sense of loyalty.

I'd watch the schoolteacher during our daily lessons. I'd watch the way the breeze pushed our shirts to the side, but it could never muster enough power to sway her thick garments. Her hair was tied back and buried in a head-cap. Except for the stray strands that attempted a desperate escape at the top of her head, I'd never seen her hair. Her shirt, tucked and secure, was the color of cream, and its sleeves and neckline covered all exposed skin. Her skirt skimmed the ground when she walked. It was navy blue and looked far too warm for even a breezy spring day. In fact, everything about her looked...weird.

It was safe to say I didn't care for her much.

I didn't like that she dressed weird, and I didn't like that she was mean. Her rules were strange, and she threatened to punish anyone who didn't follow them. It didn't take long for me to hear the snap of her whip in my dreams.

I didn't care much for the pastor, either. I'd hated him

from the moment I'd met him. There was an arrogance in the way he talked, carried himself. He strolled when he walked, as though he didn't have a care in the world.

I'd never told Mother or Father my feelings, even after I'd started noticing them whispering to each other in corners and behind doors. I pretended everything was okay.

Smack!

I heard the stark slap of the wood before I understood what had happened, but then I felt it. The pressure building along my bare inner thigh. It radiated from me, pulsing in stinging waves of sheer discomfort. I'd been sitting cross-legged, but now, every nerve in my body was telling me to flail about. The pain was excruciating.

I cried out and cowered as a hand came down, blocking the sun from my eyes. Her eyes were wild, dark, and full of hunger. She enjoyed the pain she inflicted, and I was beginning to understand why she had no job teaching in the other world.

The stick she used to whip me snapped, pieces falling to the ground beside me. Tears burned as I dug my fingers into the soil I sat atop. Crying showed weakness, and I wouldn't grant her that pleasure.

I could no longer hear the peaceful sounds of nature. The birds no longer chirped. The wind no longer fluttered through the trees' leaves. Even the sounds of insects fell silent. All I could hear was my heart in my head, and it ached, begging to be released.

CHAPTER TWO

I loved the way her nose crinkled when she was choosing the perfect color. I loved the way her brows furrowed when she was concentrating on the next stroke. I loved the way she sighed when it all came together. But most of all, I loved that she was painting again.

It had taken countless nights of lost sleep, appointments with a celebrity guru therapist, and more than a year's time, but Jezebel was slowly becoming her former self. The quick-witted, smart-talking woman I'd fallen in love with despite my every effort not to.

The locks clicked closed, and I typed in the security password on the alarm system. I smiled internally, thinking about the day I'd installed the system. She had insisted we choose 1-2-3-4-5-6 as the password. Her reasoning? Because it was ridiculous. No one would try it. I shook my head, suppressing a chuckle.

Apartments in New York City were small, but Jezebel had managed to score the perfect place with this brownstone. She loved it. I could tell by the look on her face when she'd offered me a tour of my new home. As her bodyguard, I had been hired to protect her from a stalker, and part of the deal was that I lived with her until he was caught.

Brent Miller.

Brent Fucking Miller.

His name made my veins ice. I exhaled slowly, my fists squeezed at my sides. I hated him, but I hated myself most of all. I'd promised her I'd protect her from him, and even though he'd met his fate, I still hated knowing he'd gotten as close to her as he had.

I shrugged off my jacket and folded it over the back of the barstool chair by the kitchen counter. Without a formal dining area, we often ate here. Jezebel once teased that, in time, we'd do other—much naughtier—things on this very counter.

But that was before.

Before Brent Miller abducted her.

Before Brent Miller nearly raped her.

Before Brent Miller wormed his way into her soul, burrowing deeply, forever changing her.

For many months after her return to me, she'd slept in the bedroom closet. I'd slept upright, my back to the wall beside the closed and locked door between us, my gun in its holster, clipped to my pants. She'd never admitted it, but she'd feared being alone with me while she slept. She'd feared being alone with *anyone* while she'd slept, so I'd installed a lock on her closet door, and she'd kept the world at bay, sleeping with the door locked and the light on.

After several months, she'd slowly emerged from the closet, returning to her bed. I'd remained on the floor, but this time, I'd positioned myself between her and the bedroom door. After a few weeks, I'd woken to find her nestled beside me, her head on my lap, shivering without a blanket. I'd carried her to bed, tucking her in. Before I could return to the floor, she'd woken, grabbed my hand, and beckoned me to sleep beside her.

A year after Jezebel's abduction, I'd begun to see the brazen woman I fell in love with. There was a spark in her eyes, in the way she watched me move. I'd find her gnawing her lower lip, her eyes trailing my frame. I was terrified of returning those glances. While I yearned to touch her again, the thought of rushing her recovery made me feel ill.

We'd had sex exactly one time since her abduction, and it was like nothing we'd ever experienced before. Usually a take-charge woman, she'd offered me the reins, and slowly, I'd made love to her. I'd touched her softly, sweetly. I'd kissed the scars *he* had left on her. But that was weeks ago.

Usually, she painted in the spare bedroom, which served as her writing office and art studio, but today, sprawled on the floor, paint swatches scattered about, she was in the living room. She glanced up, smiling.

"I smell Chinese," she said, inhaling dramatically. She stood, wiping her hands together as she trudged toward me.

"Chicken Mei Fun," I said, pulling out the carton of noodles from the bag. Her eyes lit up, just as I knew they would. It didn't take me long to learn her favorites from every local restaurant. Jezebel was a habitual eater, and that made my job as her bodyguard much easier. "And spring rolls with extra sauce on the side."

She exhaled sharply, her hand over her chest as she squeezed her eyes shut. "A man after my heart."

I arched a brow. "I thought I already had that."

She smiled widely, closing the space between us. Standing on her tiptoes, she placed a gentle kiss to my lips before turning on her heels to face what she really wanted: dinner.

"Chopsticks? Score!"

"No plates tonight?" I asked, already knowing the answer.

She shook her head, turning toward the sink to wash her hands. I grabbed two wineglasses, poured generous splashes into each one, and carried them to the living room.

"How was work?" she asked as I set up our dinner on the coffee table.

"Good. I think I've found some temporary bodyguard work in the city."

"Really? That's great! Where?" she asked as she dried her hands with a towel. She hung it on its hook and walked toward me.

"There's a small startup that's looking for experienced guards. They cater to celebrities and the wealthy staying in the city short-term. New York is perfect for this kind of work."

She smiled. I knew saying that would make her happy. When she hired me, we'd talked about moving, but she loved Manhattan. Even though she'd known it was risky, her stubbornness had prevailed; she would not move. Now that that fucker was gone for good, she would breathe easier, and I could start settling down in the city. While I was still technically her bodyguard, she didn't really need my services anymore. And if I had to sit through another weekday *Gilmore Girls* marathon with her, I'd go crazy, so I'd started looking for work that would get me out of the house while not keeping me too far away from Jezebel.

She flopped onto the couch beside me and slurped her noodles from her chopsticks. Jezebel was a food junkie. She could dive into her meal and completely finish before ever realizing she'd forgotten to turn on the TV, which, let's be honest, was the whole point of eating in the living room. I suppressed a smile after she moaned while eating.

I turned on the TV and froze in fear when I saw the news

headline.

As a marine and as a bodyguard, I'd often faced dire circumstances. My decisions had resulted in loss of life. But rarely had I ever felt that feeling of utter dread when your heart seemingly stops beating yet your blood is rushing to your head. That moment of complete shock and fear when you know your world is about to end and all you can do is sit and watch it happen.

But I felt it now.

"Once again, for those just tuning in, two bodies have been found deep in the woods. Witnesses discovered the graves while hiking pine plantations near Morgan Hill State Park in upstate New York. More on this breaking story..."

My chest clenched, and I felt like I was really, truly dying. I'd come close to dying before, and my career wasn't exactly gentle on my soul, but I'd never feared death. Then again, I'd never feared life either.

"You okay, babe?" Jezebel asked.

I swallowed the knot in my throat and nodded. "Piece of chicken lodged in my throat. I'm okay."

She rubbed my back, trying to soothe my pain. I loved her caring nature. She was a spitfire most times, and it was rare when she showed how gentle a soul she actually was. But now, in this moment, I fought the urge to slap away her hand. Not because I wanted to but because I wasn't sure I could lie if she asked one more time.

"How about a movie?" I asked, hitting the button that silenced the news and turned on Netflix.

★ ★ ★

She grabbed me by the hands, walking backward as she led us toward our bedroom. The glimmer in her eyes told me everything I needed to know. Excitement grew and threatened to bubble over, but I suppressed the urge to succumb to my giddiness.

When we made it to the bedroom, she gracefully slid her way onto the bed. I hadn't noticed how nearly naked she was. In just a tank top and shorts, she was absolutely breathtaking. Her legs were long, lean, and pale, and I craved to run my hand up the length of them.

Her abductor had scarred her body, but even more devastatingly, he'd ruined her confidence. Though she no longer found herself beautiful, the changes to her body didn't thwart me or my near-constant erection whenever she was around.

She faced me, frozen, her breath coming in quick, short bursts as I stared down at her. It had been so long since we'd bared ourselves to each other, and I could see how nervous she was. It hit me like a knife to the heart. More than anything, I hated how he'd changed her beautiful, confident soul.

I kicked off my shoes, yanked off my shirt, and unbuttoned my jeans, letting them fall to the floor. Kicking my clothes to the side, I stood in only boxer briefs. I descended toward her, crawling until my lips reached hers. She latched on to me, seemingly needing this contact as much as I did.

Her mouth opened to mine, and she swallowed my moans. The smooth caresses quickly turned fierce, and I found myself stripping her of her clothes until she was bare beneath me. Hiking up her legs, she removed my boxers with her feet, and I chuckled into her mouth.

"Can't wait to get me naked, love?" I joked.

She reached down and grasped me. I was already impossibly hard, but I felt myself growing beneath her touch. I was sure I'd scream if I wasn't inside her soon.

I angled my hips, lodging at her entrance. She was slick, and as I swiveled my hips, she coated me with her wetness.

"Are you sure?" I asked as I slowed my pace.

She nodded. "I want this. I want you."

Slowly, I slid into her. She gasped as I widened her tight entrance. I was thick and long, and I was sure I was bigger than most, so I restrained myself by digging my fingers into the mattress each time I wanted to slam into her.

She moaned beneath me as I slowly moved just inside her. In and out. In and out. The pace was excruciating. I was desperate to feel her quiver as I took her fully. I needed to feel her dig her nails into my back as she held on to me. Her gasps were enough to make me come.

"Faster," she whispered, eyes closed.

I quickened my pace, offering another inch. She arched her back as I pushed inside her. She was impossibly tight and so fucking hot. Her pussy grasped each inch of my cock as I slid into her. I couldn't stop myself. I pulled out completely and then slammed back into her, offering her my full length.

"Fuck!" she cried.

I supported my weight on one arm, using the other hand to play with her clit. She was soaked, and my fingers slipped off and on the tiny bud.

"Yes, please. Just like that."

Her back was arched, her neck angled so she stared at the corner of the ceiling. I pumped in and out of her, watching the expressions cross her face as I fucked her.

Angling my hips, I rubbed against the spot deep within

her that would make her come over and over again for me.

"James," she said, breathless. I knew she was close.

"Come with me," I said, my voice gruff as my orgasm reached its peak.

She tightened around me, her pussy gripping my dick so hard I was sure it'd break off. She breathed my name as she came, and I felt myself empty inside her. Her body shook beneath mine as I held her close, my cock still twitching with aftershocks.

CHAPTER THREE

The aroma of coffee filled the apartment. Normally, I was a light sleeper and woke with every little noise, but last night, I slept like the dead. Tornado sirens wouldn't have woken me.

I dragged myself out of bed and walked into the bathroom, yawing and staring at myself in the mirror while I waited for the sink water to warm. I replayed last night over and over again as I brushed my teeth. I tried to shake away the memories of being inside Jezebel. My morning wood already ached, begging for a release, and at this rate, I'd be stroking in the shower.

I had to focus on something other than my dick. What was on today's calendar? Jezebel was working on her next book today, but maybe she and I could get lunch. I dropped my rinsed toothbrush into the holder and went searching for her. Some sort of plan would help before I showered.

I turned the corner to walk into the kitchen and came to a screeching halt. Jezebel was facing the coffeemaker, pouring herself a cup. Her legs, long and lean, were bare. She wore nothing but one of my button-up dress shirts, and I was fairly confident that if she reached for another mug, her ass would be bare too.

"Morning," she said without looking back.

I tried to speak but couldn't find the words. I cleared my throat, and she turned to face me. I inhaled sharply. "Christ,

Jezebel."

"Hmm?" she asked as she took a sip of her coffee, completely unaware of her effect on me.

"Are you trying to kill me?" I asked. I scanned the length of her body, settling on her half-assed attempt at buttoning my shirt. She'd only managed to link a few, leaving a rather revealing view of her breasts. The longer I stared at her, the harder her nipples grew. And I was right—she wasn't wearing *anything* but my shirt.

For fuck's sake. I came to her to distract myself from beating my shit in the shower.

She smiled a devilish grin, and I was done. I strode toward her and then tossed her mug into the sink behind her, not caring if it was strong enough to withstand such abuse. I tangled my hand in her hair, pulling her to me. We crushed our lips together as she leaned against me—and then our tongues.

I reached down, gripped her ass, and lifted her into the air. She wrapped her legs around me, and I set her down atop the counter. I made a sad attempt to unbutton my favorite work shirt but ended up gripping the fabric and yanking it free. Buttons clattered to the ground, and the shirt landed beside them in a heap.

"You're so fucking sexy right now," she said as I kissed her neck.

I grumbled something I knew she couldn't understand as I palmed her breast. Her nipple was rock hard beneath my hand. It was begging to be touched. I knew that feeling well.

She leaned back until she was resting on her elbows, which gave me perfect access to her chest. I placed a hand on her back and pulled her toward me as I explored her body with my other. Her skin was soft beneath my palm as I rubbed each and every crevice.

I latched on to her nipple and rubbed the hardened bud with my tongue. With each moan that escaped her lips, I sucked harder. I nipped her breast just as my hand reached her clit. A surge of her wetness coated my fingers.

I focused on her other nipple as I inserted a finger into her.

"Yes," she breathed.

I slid in and out, slowly, carefully, until she was desperate for more attention. I added another digit and pulled away from her breasts. She leaned forward, kissing me, sucking on my lips as I fucked her with my hand.

"I want to taste you," I said.

She hiked up her legs until her heels rested on the edge of the countertop. I pulled out my fingers and brought them to my mouth, sucking her juices.

"That's so fucking hot," she said, her voice deep with passion.

I smiled and splayed her open to me. Sucking on my bottom lip, I stared at her pussy. It was still plump from being fucked last night and then teased this morning. I could smell her arousal, and it smelled like heaven. Her musk was sweet yet earthy, and I could've dined on it all damn day.

I leaned in and swiped my tongue up the length of her pussy, teasing her clit with the tip when I reached the end. I sucked her into my mouth and relished her taste as she squirmed beneath me.

I licked her again, this time sinking my tongue into her.

"Oh, yes," she whispered. "Fuck me like that, James."

And I did. I fucked her until my tongue couldn't thrust anymore. When I sucked on her clit again, she came in my mouth, and I swallowed everything she gave me. Pulling back, I wiped my mouth with the back of my hand and stroked my dick.

Her eyes were lidded. I knew she was still riding her orgasm, so I quickly positioned myself and sank deep inside her.

She cried out, her pussy clenching my dick. I thrust long and hard, grabbing the flesh of her ass as I worked myself toward my own release.

"Rub your clit," I ordered. I watched myself move in and out of her in quick thrusts as she struggled to rub herself.

"I'm going to come again," she said.

I nodded, even though she couldn't see me; she still hadn't opened her eyes from her last orgasm.

My abs strained as I thrust into her over and over again, feeling my release closing in. Just as I was about to come, I felt her tighten around me, clenching my dick in an ironclad grasp that squeezed my own orgasm from me.

I leaned against her as we caught our breaths. I listened to her heartbeat until it slowed to normal, and then I stood back. I was still inside her, but I'd almost completely deflated. Pulling out, I watched as my come seeped from her swollen, fire-red pussy.

"I never get tired of seeing that," I said.

She smiled and kissed me. It was a soft, sweet kiss that left me breathless.

"Join me in the shower?"

She shook her head. "Too much to do, and I already showered."

"But you're dirty again," I crooned.

"I'll clean myself up while you shower, and then we can

eat breakfast together before I leave."

"Or we can skip breakfast and take a long, hot soak in the hot tub."

There was a hot tub on the rooftop, which was our own private space. Jezebel didn't use the hot tub nearly enough, but the weather today was perfect.

She bit her lip. "You know I'd love that, but I can't today. I have to write, and then I have that meeting with Tara. Rain check?"

"I'll hold you to that, Miss Tate."

While Jezebel retreated to the bathroom to clean herself, I cleaned up our mess. As I was picking up my clothes, the television grabbed my attention. I hadn't even realized it was on. The morning anchor was talking about a recent string of murders in the area. It had nothing to do with my parents, but I couldn't stop my thoughts from flickering to them. Soon, the world would know what had happened, and I wasn't sure I was prepared for that.

I sauntered into the bathroom as Jezebel retreated toward the bedroom to change. Tossing the dirty clothes into the hamper, I stepped into the shower and turned on the faucet. The water felt great, but it wasn't hot enough. I adjusted the handle until it was nearly scalding, providing the perfect amount of pain and pressure on my skin. It was the ideal distraction to avoid thinking about my fucked-up past.

Lather. Rinse. Repeat. I mindlessly shuffled through my morning routine, thinking of pointless facts to keep myself occupied.

I wouldn't let my past come back to bite me in the ass, to ruin everything I'd built for myself since I left Living Light.

But everywhere I turned, I saw evidence of my demons

washing ashore, clinging to my heels as I unsuccessfully trudged through the sand in my escape. I was ankle-deep now, and soon, almost as if some long-buried psychic abilities were resurfacing, I knew this quicksand would have me by the throat.

After my shower, I dressed in jeans and a T-shirt, re-brushed my teeth, ignored my five o'clock shadow, and went in search of Jezebel. She sat cross-legged on the couch in the living room, the television on, her eyes locked on the screen as she sipped coffee from a mug Tara, her agent and best friend, got her for Christmas last year. The text on the side read *This isn't coffee*. She laughed for a good twenty minutes when she unwrapped it. I smiled as I thought of that day. It was after her attack, and in that moment, the old Jezebel shined through the darkness that surrounded her. It was brief, but she was there. I yearned to grab her and block that darkness from ever suffocating her again.

"Breakfast?" I asked.

She didn't respond as I grabbed the carton of eggs and a package of bacon. I glanced at the clock. Soon, she'd leave for the café to work on her next book. She was excited about it, but she never talked to anyone about the plot. When I'd asked why she wouldn't share the details with me, she'd said she was trying to be secretive. Norman Mailer, an American novelist, had explained once in a stiff, scripted interview scene on *Gilmore Girls*—Jezebel's favorite television show—that secrecy was important to the creative process.

I scrambled our eggs in a bowl before splashing them into the pan. The bacon was sizzling beside them, offering a mouthwatering aroma. I loved the smell of good food cooking in the kitchen. So did Jezebel, but whatever she was watching on TV had captured her attention to the point of blissful ignorance. It was as if I wasn't even here.

"Jez," I called, chuckling internally when I received no response.

I scooped our servings onto plates and brought them into the living room. I placed hers below her chin, letting the steam waft toward her. Her eyes grew wide as she set her mug down and accepted my offering.

"Smells delicious," she said, licking her lips.

I ignored the twitch in my cock as she did so and cleared my throat.

"I hope you're hungry for eggs and bacon. You didn't hear me earlier."

"Sorry. They're talking about those bodies they found," she said, nodding toward the TV.

Everything silenced save for the newscaster. She was as loud as an air horn in a library.

"I guess those hikers were just walking their dogs in the woods, and that's how they found 'em." She took a bite of eggs. "Apparently, there's evidence of a community there. Locals didn't even know about it. They're calling it a cult. I guess there were remnants of religious relics. Crazy, huh? I mean, this clearly has the makings for a Hollywood blockbuster."

I listened as the news anchor explained that local authorities were still investigating the possible crime. I was so consumed by what I was sure to be the reporting of my parents' bodies, I didn't hear Jezebel's cell phone ring.

"Hello?" she said. A few seconds passed. "Hello!" She hung up.

"No one there?" I whispered, almost unable to speak.

She shook her head, visibly shaken, obviously reliving a

memory of the time she'd been taken. I wasn't an idiot. In fact, I was fantastic at reading people. I'd made a career from my keen ability to break through the bullshit. She was helpless when it happened, and even though he was gone for good, anytime she experienced even a second of vulnerability, she relived her abduction.

I wanted to console her. I *needed* to console her, but I couldn't focus. The world was dangerously close to discovering my past, so I was a man torn between two instincts: flight or fight.

CHAPTER FOUR

After Jezebel left to spend the day writing at the café, I opened my laptop and typed in the website address I'd become all too familiar with. The design was simple, focusing almost solely on her blog.

Abigail wrote near-daily posts about her father's involvement in my family's death. Every time I read the words "the *true* story," I wanted to slam my laptop against the wall. I'd fought this urge for years, but now I was beginning to wonder how much longer I could deny the impulse.

I clicked on the website's About page and waited for it to load. My foot tapped uncontrollably against the hardwood floors as my gaze flickered to the door. Jezebel hadn't been gone even fifteen minutes. She'd be working on her book all morning and well into the afternoon, and even though I knew this, my paranoia was all-consuming.

I glanced back at my laptop's screen and inhaled sharply. The woman in the photo stared back at me. She leaned against a tree, her arms casually crossed over her chest. The camera's lens had focused on her, but a color-speckled field was blurred behind her. She smiled widely. It was a knowing smile, and it wasn't for the camera that was surely clipped to a tripod a few feet away from her. She smiled for me, and even though I'd seen this photo hundreds of times, it still took away my breath.

Because I knew that color-speckled field of wildflowers in the distance.

I knew the thick base of the weeper she leaned against.

I could almost hear the way its branches swayed in the breeze, even now, even from where I sat hundreds of miles away.

She smiled for me because she knew I'd recognize the location of her staged photo, and it made my blood boil every time I saw it.

Abigail. I never knew her last name. Living Light wasn't exactly a community for people concerned about logistics, so when she and her father showed up seeking refuge, they were welcomed with open arms. We were naïve, yes, but that was our way; everyone was given a chance. I didn't think much of her when we first met, but I certainly didn't see then what I saw now. I wish I had. One of the first skills I honed in my years of Spec Ops was how to spot evil. Honestly, it just made the job easier if I could look at my target and sense a killer. If only it'd been a natural-born talent...

I stared at her picture and watched as she slowly morphed into a demon that'd clearly escaped the depths of hell. After all, it took a spectacularly psychotic person to condone the actions of the man who murdered an entire group of people.

She looked almost identical to the girl I once knew. Her skin pale, her eyes a light blue, her hair a faded shade of red. She was average in every aspect.

I scrolled to the website's footer and noted the viewer log. Exhaling slowly, I added the new number and today's date in the log I had been keeping in a password-protected document on my laptop. It seemed I was the only one viewing this horrid site. As much as I'd like it to stay that way, I couldn't help the gnawing feeling in my gut whenever I glanced at the television. With the bodies piling up, there's no way this site wouldn't make waves.

Eventually, the world would discover it. Jezebel would discover my truth, and I was sure she would leave forever.

I slammed closed my laptop, not even bothering to exit out of the website I'd been stalking. I stomped down the hall and tossed the computer atop the chest of drawers. I strummed my fingers against the wooden top, knowing what I needed to do but dreading making the call.

My phone buzzed in my pocket. I pulled it out and read a text from Jezebel.

Writing's not going well.

I frowned.

Why?

Trying to write a sex scene in a coffee shop full of stay-at-home moms with babies screaming all around me...

Yikes.

How about some inspiration?

I grinned at the winky-face emoji that followed her

request.

*Have you always been
such a shameless minx?*

No. You ruined me.

I swallowed hard. She didn't know then how true that statement would become.

Don't go soft on me, Blakeley.

Another winky face, followed by a couple of crying-while-laughing ones. I shook my head. She definitely loved her emojis. My phone lit up with a new message, and my dick nearly sprang from my pants.

*I want to watch you jack off while
all these oppressed housewives secretly
wish they were watching someone as
sexy as you stroke that D.*

Jezebel...

I was already painfully hard. My dick pressed against my jeans, and I shifted to ease the sting. Already, my crotch was peaked like some fucked-up tent.

I'm not kidding, B. Strip. Now.

I slipped out of my jeans, thankful for the release of pressure, and climbed onto the bed. I snapped a picture of my dick, still in my boxer briefs, and sent it to Jezebel, knowing my hard-on was obvious and in full force.

Holy fuck. More.

I slid my boxers down to my knees, and my dick sprang free. I snapped another picture, knowing she'd appreciate this one much more than the other. Long, thick, and pointing toward the ceiling, my cock was ready to sink into something soft and sweet. Sadly, at this rate, that something would be my hand, and my hand was nowhere near as soft and sweet as Jezebel's tight, wet pussy.

Stroke. Your. Dick.

I laughed. I loved her dirty mouth. Before I could snap another picture, my screen lit up with a video-call. I answered.

"Are you really video-calling me right now?" I said, unable to contain my smile.

"Relax. My headphones are in, and I'm at a corner table."

I didn't have to look past her silhouette to know that was true. Ever since her attack, she watched her surroundings, choosing corner booths over center tables everywhere we went. She once told me her attacker surprised her by cornering her, and I knew this was her way of ensuring that never happened again. I loved that she was more careful now, but I hated it was because of what he did to her. Her confidence and security had been crushed.

"You're insatiable," I said.

"I'm...in need of inspiration," she said, smiling. "Show me."

I flipped the camera's lens so it was focused on the view in front of me, which currently consisted of my hand wrapped around the base of my dick. Jezebel moaned softly as I stroked, slowly at first, hoping it'd tease her. I watched her face on the screen, my dick growing harder as she gnawed on her lower lip, her eyes focused on my every movement.

"Are you sure you can't come home early?" I asked.

She grinned and tapped on the screen. When she looked back at me, my phone beeped.

*Why? What would you
do to me if I was there?*

I smiled. "You know *exactly* what I'd do to you if you were here."

She groaned, rolling her eyes.

"You want details?" I teased.

She nodded enthusiastically.

"First, I'd strip you of those clothes. They'd definitely be in the way."

She giggled, finally releasing her lower lip from her clenched teeth. It was red, plump, and it made my dick ache. I wanted to do so many things to that mouth. I wanted to suck on her lip until her sensitive skin couldn't take it anymore. I'd bite the skin there until she cried out. I wanted to shove my dick down her throat and watch as she took me as far as she could. I'd run my hands through her silky hair as I pushed her to every limit she had. I wanted to show her how amazing sex could be. But I knew I could never be that rough with her. Not anymore. Not after what had happened.

Keep going. I'm so wet.

Groaning, I grasped my dick harder. Trying to ease the urgency to throw on clothes, run to the café, and fuck her where she sat, I squeezed the head of my dick so hard it was almost painful.

"Tell me what you'd do," she whispered.

"I'd slide into your mouth, letting your tongue get me good and wet. I'd watch as you sucked every drop of pre-come I gave you. And you'd like it, wouldn't you?"

"Yes," she said. Her breath hitched, and her chest was heaving. I knew she was aroused, so I kept going.

"I'd push into that tight cunt fast and hard." I quickened my pace and tightened my grip.

Her skin flushed, and I was sure her panties were soaked.

"I'd fuck you until you screamed my name, until you came so fucking hard you weren't sure you'd ever stop coming."

She squirmed in her seat and closed her eyes. I imagined her squeezing her legs together, hoping for any kind of pressure she could give her throbbing clit right now.

"After you came, I'd pull out and suck your swollen clit into my mouth, taking my time, giving you orgasm after orgasm until you couldn't take it anymore, until you were too sensitive and begged me to stop. You'd feel what I'd do to you for days after I was done fucking you."

She inhaled sharply, and I thought about continuing. I was eager to see if I could make her come with just my words and the image of me rubbing my dick while thinking about her pussy.

This is so fucking hot. I want you. Now.

And I came. Hard. Fast. I came in hot, milky streaks that shot out and landed on my chest. I moaned my release and told her I wished she were here. I wished I'd made her come with me.

"I wish I were there, baby," she said. She placed two fingers to her lips, kissed them, and then brought them to the screen. I loved when she did that. It was raw, honest, real, yet so terrifying. It was a gesture of true love, and my chest ached every time she showed me such care.

"I love you," I said.

"I love you, too." She smiled. "Join me for lunch?"

I nodded, promised I'd be there soon, and hung up. With a new sense of determination, I cleaned up, zipped up my pants, pulled out my phone, and finished what I started the moment I'd discovered the website all those years ago.

CHAPTER FIVE

I didn't want to go to the pastor's house for dinner. I didn't want to meet his daughter, Abigail, and I certainly didn't want to give up the few hours I had to play with my friends after chores were done.

"James," Mother said, her voice strained. I knew she was holding back a whoopin', so I stopped whining. Maybe if I ate quickly, we'd be back home before the sun set, and I could still play outside.

I combed my hair to the side, pretending not to hear my parents whispering.

"Are we sure about this?" Mother asked. "We barely know them."

"You needn't worry, sweetheart. We must think of the good of the community. He brings a wealth of knowledge. Everyone is placed in the area of his or her strength. You know this." I watched as Father brushed a hair from Mother's face, tucking it behind her ear. She smiled.

"But power over the entire community? How do we know he won't ruin everything we built?" she asked. She frowned. It was unnatural for her, and it made me grimace. Mother was always happy. The only time I'd seen her cry was when someone left to be with God, and even then, her pain was brief.

"We've always said that God has brought us all together for a reason. Who's to say God didn't bring him to us too?"

Mother exhaled slowly, but before she could respond, her gaze flickered to mine. I turned away quickly, as if I hadn't just been caught eavesdropping.

"We'll discuss this later," she said quickly. I heard her approach, so I ran to my bedroom and jumped on my bed, pretending I'd been reading my Bible the whole time. It didn't take her long to find me. "Come, James. We'll be late."

As we stepped outside, the breeze fluffed my hair. I groaned and combed it back to the side with my fingers. I scanned my surroundings, looking for my friends.

The community was small, and the houses were built closely together in the living quarters. Every house at Living Light looked the same, with stairs leading to the front door. Each cabin was raised for fear of flooding. With each passing year, the wood used to build the homes grayed, leaving no remnants of the light-cream color it used to be.

We arrived at the pastor's house minutes after leaving our own. A line of stones led to the pastor's door. I skipped my way toward his house, hopping from one slab to the next. When we reached the door, I knocked, standing in front of my parents. Quickly, I ran a hand through my hair once more, sure the welcome summer breeze had made a mess of it once again.

"Welcome!" the pastor said after opening the door.

My stomach grumbled, and my heart shook. The pastor made me feel uneasy. I wasn't sure what it was about him that I disliked, but being near him made my skin crawl. No one else seemed to be afflicted, so I ignored my instincts and offered a fake, wide smile whenever I saw him. He always looked at me strangely, as if he knew I didn't like him. Maybe he didn't like me either.

My parents and I filed inside. I shook his hand and mumbled a greeting, but I was more interested in snooping around his house. No one had been invited in after he moved here. I was sure he was hiding something.

My gaze landed on a girl. She was young, like me, and pretty. Her hair was light red, and her skin was pale. I wondered if he kept her inside all the time. She walked over to me and offered a small wave.

"I'm Abigail," she said quietly.

"James."

Her eyes were light blue, kind of like mine. She had freckles on her skin that seemed to disappear when she crinkled her nose.

"What's that smell?" Abigail asked.

The pastor laughed. It was a bellowed sound that seemed to shake the walls. I narrowed my eyes. Even his laugh sounded fake. "I should have warned you that I'm not much of a chef."

My parents laughed, but their laughter also sounded forced. Was no one happy to be here?

"I'm sure it's wonderful," Mother said, her lips in a firm smile. Why was she acting so...weird? Did she not like him either? "Can I help with anything?"

"No, no. You're my guest. Come, join me at the table. Abigail, have you finished your chores?"

"Yes, Father."

"Perhaps you and James would like to retire to the living area?"

I gasped. I was sure my eyes would pop right out of my head. I didn't want to spend any time alone with her, but Mother would be upset if I made a scene. I watched as my parents joined the pastor at his table, leaving me alone with

Abigail.

"Living room is this way," she said, walking in the opposite direction of my parents and the door to escape this mess.

I didn't want to go with her. I didn't want to make a new friend. I groaned internally, crossing my arms over my chest.

Exhaling sharply, I followed Abigail into the living room and sat on the floor in the center of the small room. If I turned, I could see my parents speaking to the pastor in hushed tones. Mother looked upset, and Father had wrapped his arm around her shoulders. Her skin was flushed, and her hands were balled into fists.

I turned back toward Abigail. She was sitting on the floor beside me, pulling her knees to her chest. She wrapped her arms around her legs and slowly rocked side to side. Her dress was long, and the bottom skidded against the wood floors. I sat straighter and watched the wall in front of us.

"I like your dress," I said robotically, not looking at her. I thought it was blue, but the dim light in the room might have played tricks on me. All I knew for sure was that blue was my favorite color.

"Thanks," she said quietly.

"I like your house," I added.

"Me too."

"Do you like living here?" I glanced at her. I liked to ask people this question, because everyone always seemed to love it here just as much as I did. But Abigail was new, and she didn't know anyone besides her father. Maybe they hated it here. Maybe they'd leave.

She shrugged. "I don't want to marry you. Can I stay if I don't marry you?"

This time, I turned to face her fully. "Huh?"

"Father said we have to get married, but I don't want to. He said he's telling your parents tonight."

I frowned. "But I don't want to be married."

"Don't tell him that. He gets...angry when you disobey him."

Only then did I notice the bruises on her arm, as if someone had grabbed her too tightly. I reached forward and touched them with my fingertips. She shivered and pulled away, yanking her sleeves down to cover the marks.

"Why do we have to get married?" I asked, not really sure what it meant to be married. My parents were married, and I loved my parents. Maybe I could love being married too?

She shrugged again. "God says so."

I nodded. "Then we should. God wants us to, and we always do what God wants. I mean, God is never wrong, right?"

She giggled. "Wrong right?"

We both laughed but were quickly silenced when the pastor called us to join them at the table.

CHAPTER SIX

I glanced at the clock. Half past noon. The café Jezebel writes at was a short walk down the street. I'd be there in less than five minutes if I left now, but before I could join her, I needed to finish what I'd started. I grabbed my phone, scrolled through its contacts list, and clicked to call a friend.

"Blakely, as I live and breathe. How've you been, man?" a familiar voice asked.

"Reynolds. Good. You?"

"Can't complain. How's the contractor life?"

"Good money. Ready to accept my offer yet?" I asked. It was a loaded question. I knew Reynolds wouldn't leave his desk job for the life I now lived. He was ready to leave behind a life of excitement and unpredictability for the stability his nine-to-five offered his family.

"The money isn't so bad here," he said.

"Glad to hear that. How are the girls?" I asked.

"Monica stays at home now. She loves it. We've taken Bethany out of daycare. My in-laws are thrilled," he said with a groan.

"I'm surprised your mother-in-law hasn't enrolled her in an online home school program already. I'm sure those have wait lists." I laughed.

His in-laws were constantly trying to meddle in his parenting. He hated it, but he never complained. He was just happy to have made it home alive from the military. Putting in a decade more than me, Reynolds was the first to admit he was ready to retire. His confession was what had prompted everyone to reject contract renewals.

"She sends me brochures weekly."

I could practically hear him roll his eyes. He'd always wanted the best for Bethany, but that meant dealing with his in-laws on a daily basis now. Monica was trying to get pregnant again, without success, and everyone seemed to have an opinion on how he should raise the child they already had.

"In-laws," I nagged.

"How's Jezebel?" he asked.

"Better," I said simply. I never offered more than short, vague answers when it came to her recovery, both as a courtesy to her and an obligation to my profession. I trusted Reynolds with my life and secrets, but I wouldn't betray her trust.

"Good. Glad to hear it. You know I followed the news stories. I can't tell you how many times I almost contacted the guys. We would've been there in under an hour to take care of the problem."

I smiled. I'd retired from the marines almost two years ago, and before I met Jezebel, I struggled with the decision to walk away. After my parents' death, they were the only family I knew. It was hard to go from seeing them daily to just exchanging emails. Nevertheless, even though we rarely saw each other, we were still family. I would die for them. They would kill for me. And I knew by "take care of the problem," he meant no one would ever find Brent Miller's body. In these moments, I never knew what to say. Words couldn't express the love we shared. The bond shared by the brotherhood in this life was unbreakable.

"As much as I love just listening to you breathe, I should get back to work," he joked.

I grinned. "I need a favor."

"Name it."

"I need some information on a girl. First name Abigail. Alfa. Bravo. India. Golf. Alfa. India. Lima. I don't have a last name, but I have a website. Maybe you can link back to the source? Track her down for me?"

"Website?"

"Living Light Massacre. Lima, India, Victor, India, November, Golf, Lima, India, Golf, Hotel, Tango, Mike, Alfa, Sierra, Sierra, Alfa, Charlie, Romeo, Echo..."

"Got it," he confirmed after I relayed the entire web address. "Give me an hour."

I thanked him, hung up, and locked the door behind me as I left the apartment to meet Jezebel for lunch.

I hadn't seen my unit in over a year, choosing to skip our yearly retreat in order to stay with Jezebel during her recovery. We shared emails and text messages often, but it wasn't the same. During Jezebel's attack, she'd suffered severe wounds. Her brain had taken the worst of it, though, and she'd fallen into a coma. The doctor had assured me this wasn't exactly out of the norm, but when I'd shared the news with Reynolds, he'd shown up at the hospital. It wasn't an easy trek from North Carolina to where we were in Maine, but I hadn't been surprised to see him at her door when someone knocked.

I'd never told Jezebel—mainly because he'd shown up to do what he thought I was too busy to do: kill Miller. Little did he know, Jezebel had already done the deed in an attempt to save my life. He'd stayed with me for a few days, until I forced him to leave. His family needed him more than I did.

When I reached the café, I didn't go inside. Instead, I scanned the small restaurant. I found her sitting at her usual corner table and watched her as she packed her laptop into her bag. As if she sensed my presence, she looked up, and our gazes locked. She smiled, slung her bag over her shoulder, and walked out the door and toward me.

Even now, after nearly a year and a half together, I was left awestruck by her beauty. In every way, she was stunning, from her dark-brown hair to her pale skin to her spunky heart. She was perfect.

"Hello, handsome," she said as she approached.

"Miss Tate," I said, suppressing a chuckle. She'd hated how formal I was when we'd first met, but to me, this had been just another job. Formalities were in place for a reason. Little did I know she'd worm her way into my heart. Formalities be damned.

She rolled her eyes. "I think we're on a first-name basis, Blakely. After all, I *have* seen you naked." She winked.

I reached for her and pulled her into a kiss. Her mouth was warm, inviting, and it didn't take long for the greeting to escalate. I was growing hard, every bit as hungry for her as she was for me. Reluctantly, I pulled away.

"Lunch?" she asked, breathless.

Hand in hand, we walked down the street, stealing glances as if we were truant school kids in love. We reached her favorite salad bar, Soup 'n Stuff, and in typical New York City fashion, the line to order food to go was out the door. We quickly grabbed the last empty table.

"Hollywood parking!" she said as we sat.

I grinned. "Hollywood parking" was the term Jezebel used whenever we got something only seen in movies—front-row parking on a busy street, an empty table in a packed Manhattan restaurant during the lunch hour, two full glasses of wine at an art opening...

"Were you able to finish your chapter?" I asked as I browsed the menu. We frequented this restaurant, so I'd memorized it already. Even so, I was hoping the owner would branch out. Soup, salad, and sandwiches did little to sate my appetite.

"Sure was. My inspiration break was more than helpful," she teased.

Before I could respond, the waitress was at our table, asking for our orders. She was a bubbly blonde just pushing legal drinking age. As she took our orders, her long hair, tied back in a ponytail, swayed as she looked from me to Jezebel and then back again. When Jezebel glanced down to fold her menu, the girl winked and pursed her lips, even offering me a slight head nod to the bathroom doors. I nearly strained myself in my attempt to not roll my eyes at her.

"Let me take that for you, babe," I said, grabbing our menus and handing them to the girl. I kept my focus on Jezebel, in a clear this-is-the-only-woman-I-want-to-fuck alpha stance. I was sure the waitress would get the message. Jezebel, completely unaware of the girl's advances, arched a brow at my show of dominance. It didn't take long for her to return my sexual gaze.

After she left, I threatened, "If you keep looking at me with your come-fuck-me eyes, I will take you into the bathroom, push you up against the wall, and fuck you until every person in this restaurant knows what a little minx you are."

She gasped, her cheeks flushing a bright pink. I lived for these moments. Her skin was so deliciously pale she often burned a bright pink while I fucked her, her arousal just as obvious as mine. She dragged her teeth against her lower lip. When she released it, it was plump, suckable. I licked my lips, sure that *I* now offered the come-fuck-me eyes.

"I love how naughty you can be," she whispered.

I'd never been like this. In my past relationships, I had been more reserved, but Jezebel had an insatiable sexual appetite, and I loved it. She made me want to do things to her that I'd never done before. I knew she wasn't ready for that, though, so I never pressured her to explore new things with me.

My phone buzzed, and I glanced at the screen.

"Blakely."

"Reynolds. I found your girl."

I sucked in a sharp breath. Already? That quickly? A million questions raced through my mind, but my eyes trailed the short distance to where Jezebel sat beside me. She was playing with the cuticle of her nail, pretending to not eavesdrop. Even with all my questions, I fell mute.

"Bad time?" he asked.

"Affirmative."

"Tomorrow?"

"No," I said quickly. I needed to know what he knew, and I needed to know it now.

He exhaled slowly and spoke softly, as if he feared someone might overhear him on the phone. My eyes on Jezebel, I listened as he rattled off an old address linked to her. She also had a five-year-old citation for keeping farm animals in the city. Apparently she was trying to build a small homestead in her apartment. I fought the urge to roll my eyes at that. The first clue I'd gotten that might lead to her was almost a mirror image of the life she'd stolen from me. The irony wasn't lost on me, and I was damn sure she left that citation on her record for a reason. She wanted me to find her.

Before Reynolds hung up, he told me not to fuck up things with Jezebel while I searched for this other girl. I told him I wouldn't, but mere seconds after we hung up, Jezebel asked me about the call.

"Nothing. Just helping a friend track down someone for a job."

Again, almost as if by instinct, I'd lied.

CHAPTER SEVEN

Now

As I hailed a taxi, I hated myself. In the time it had taken Jezebel and me to finish eating, I'd replayed our conversation in my mind at least a dozen times. Even after I walked her to a waiting taxi and kissed her goodbye, the only words to escape my lips were reassurance that her agent, Tara, was calling a last-minute meeting with her because she likely had good news, not bad.

I should have told her the truth about the phone call, but I couldn't bear the questions—at least, not until I knew Abigail's true intentions. I couldn't risk Jezebel's safety... Not again. With only one thought in my mind, I sent Jezebel on her way and found another taxi for myself.

"Where ya headed?" the driver asked as I slammed the car door.

I rattled off a foreign-to-me address and settled back into the seat. The skyscrapers of downtown Manhattan loomed above us as the driver sped to our destination. My mind was spinning. I had so many questions.

What was Abigail doing in Manhattan? Manhattan and Living Light couldn't be more different. Could it be a coincidence that we both ended up here? What were her intentions with her blog? Had she been involved in the discovery of my parents' bodies?

But most importantly, what would I have to do to make her, my past, and this brewing threat of exposure disappear? How far would she go to uncover my secrets?

My phone buzzed in my pocket. A text from Jezebel.

Major news, B! I'm making
dinner tonight, so don't be late.

I glanced at my wristwatch, a habit Jezebel once told me she found utterly sexy. Jezebel's meeting was over already? I'd only sent her off in the taxi twenty or so minutes ago. From the sound of it, she'd received good news. Tension I didn't realize I was holding released. At least her career was safe. Mine, on the other hand, was still a work in progress.

This sounds promising.

Yes! Can't talk. Still in meeting.

I chuckled. In typical Jezebel fashion, she was texting me dinner plans while in her business meeting with Tara. I could imagine Tara rolling her eyes and telling Jezebel to pay attention. Even though they were best friends, they were really nothing alike. Tara had the business mind, while Jezebel was driven by her emotions. I couldn't complain, though. Jezebel's emotional state led me to admit my true feelings for her. Not to mention, the sex had been spectacular.

See you later.

Before putting my phone back into my pocket, I stared at my reflection in the screen. My eyes were dark, as if I hadn't slept in a few days, and my hair was a bit messier than usual. I wasn't one to primp for hours in front of a mirror, but I usually took some care with my appearance. I smoothed the creases of my jacket and adjusted the buttons on my shirt.

We passed brownstone after brownstone. I closed my eyes in a sad attempt to shut out the world around me. I still wasn't sure what I was going to say when I saw her. Would she even recognize me? Would I recognize her? I thought about her website head shot. How long ago had she taken that photo? My mind was spinning with questions I was dying to ask her. As much as I'd have liked her to tell me she had no intention of spilling my secrets, I wasn't naïve. She was here for a reason, with a plan, and I was simply a pawn in her game.

"Sir?"

I opened my eyes.

"I said we're here."

I cleared my throat, mumbled an apology, and tossed a few twenties at him.

The sun was hot on my skin as I took the stairs to the brownstone's front door. A car alarm sounded, and I glanced in its direction, halting my ascent. The street was lined with cars. I never understood why New Yorkers kept their cars while living in the city. It just wasn't worth the expense. Insurance in this city was atrocious, and traffic was horrendous. I was almost certain you could get anywhere in this city faster by foot and public transportation.

I glanced in the other direction and watched a woman pushing a stroller as she jogged toward me. She offered a smile as she passed by, and I nodded in response. I wiped the sweat that had begun to pool on my forehead and admired the view. This street, although in another borough, looked almost identical to our street. Cars lined the curb, brownstones lined the sidewalk, and short, black, wrought-iron gates fenced in each person's property. In true New York style, there wasn't much to enclose. I shook my head, offering this similarity up to another coincidence.

When I reached the brownstone's door, I knocked. While I waited, I swallowed the lump that'd formed in my throat and tried to slow my breathing. My heart was beating so hard I could feel the pounding in my temples. I was one degree away from the worst migraine of my life. I wasn't sure what I was most nervous about—seeing Abigail again or trying to stop her from ruining my life. I'd known Abigail only a short time, but looking back, I could only assume she was psychotic. How was I going to convince a crazy person that she was crazy?

I sucked in a sharp breath as I watched a woman approach. The frosted glass of the front door made it impossible to see her clearly, but I could see she was petite. She reached for the door handle before I'd even decided what to say.

"Yes? Hello," the woman said.

She wasn't Abigail. I glanced past her, scanning the long hallway behind her. There was a staircase to the left and a row of picture frames cluttering the wall to the right.

"May I help you?" she asked.

I glanced back at her. "I was looking for a friend. I was given this address for her. Maybe you know her? Abigail..." I cleared my throat, realizing I still didn't know her last name. "Her name is Abigail."

The woman shook her head. "I'm sorry, I don't know her. My husband and I just moved in, though. We didn't meet the previous tenants prior to signing our lease."

She fidgeted with the doorframe, strumming her fingertips against the wood. Offering a weak smile, she shrugged.

"Did the previous tenant leave anything behind?" I asked, officially entering stalker status.

She exhaled slowly, her eyes straying from mine. "Look, I... I can't help you, okay?" She began to close the door, but I reached forward, blocking her escape. Her eyes widened in surprise. She leaned back, her light-brown fringe falling into her eyes. She flicked her head to the side in a mindless habit, I was sure.

"I really need to find her. Please, anything you know could be invaluable."

She frowned but said nothing. I offered a silent prayer that she was remembering something extremely useful, like a forwarding address conveniently left on the bottom stair of the apartment. I stared into her green eyes, trying to make my own look as kind as possible. The last thing I needed was a report filed with the police about some crazy man digging for information about a girl named Abigail.

"Anything at all," I repeated, smiling.

She shook her head. "Look, all I know is that the previous tenant was weird. When we moved in, the landlord was still clearing out the garbage she'd left behind. We couldn't move in on time because he had to repaint the walls. Apparently, she'd left these...I don't know, cryptic messages all over them. I'm glad I never met her, and I think you should go."

"Do you know what the messages said?" I asked.

She exhaled slowly. "I don't know. A light of the living or something like that. It was creepy, but that's all I know. Please, leave."

She pushed against the door, and I stepped back, listening as she locked the door. I heard the familiar beep of an alarm being set.

"I'm sorry," I said to the closed door. "I didn't mean to startle you."

I turned and descended the stairs. When I reached the bottom step, I ran a hand through my hair and stared at the sky. The heat was suffocating at this time of day, but I welcomed the walk home. With each step I took, a sense of dread washed over me. This address was my only lead. If I couldn't find her myself, my only choice was to wait until Abigail contacted me. That woman was right. Abigail was crazy. But maybe I was just as crazy, because I was willing to wait for her to find me.

CHAPTER EIGHT

The walk back to our house was quiet. No one spoke, but the creatures of the night helped to drown out the enveloping silence. It was late. The sun had set. The only thing lighting our way was the moon and stars, but I could walk this path blindfolded and still reach home.

As I approached our house, I looked into our neighbor's windows. The small kitchen was lit by candlelight. Bobby, my friend, was helping his mom clean up. He glanced up as we passed and waved when he saw me. I smiled and waved back. I'd missed the kickball game that day. We could only play outside until sundown, so it was too late to ask him to play now. Kicking the dirt at my feet, I hoped he'd play again tomorrow.

The door to our house slammed shut behind me, and I jumped.

"Get ready for bed, James," Mother said. I think she was upset about the pastor's news. She didn't talk much at dinner, and she wouldn't look at me after the pastor proposed my marriage to Abi.

Quickly, I took the stairs two at a time and ran into my room, not wanting to talk to my parents about dinner. I rushed my bedtime routine, eager to sleep and wake up tomorrow. Mother said I could spend the whole day outside. Soon, summer would turn to autumn, and with it, the cold would come. I didn't have many more days to play outside in the fields with my friends.

I lay in bed, tucking my blanket beneath my sides as Mother used to, and I thought about Abi. She was nice. I liked her red hair. I never knew hair could be such a light-red color. It almost looked orange. It reminded me of the sunsets. They looked orange sometimes too. Since we were getting married, maybe she'd like to play in the fields tomorrow. I could wake early and go to her house first.

Shouting from the living room jolted me from bed. My blanket tangled with my legs, and I fell to the floor in a thump. I had fallen asleep thinking about the games I'd play with Abi tomorrow. I stood and tossed the wool blanket onto the bed. Sweat coated my forehead. I liked to be warm when I slept, so I always used my winter blanket, even when it was hot outside, but I hated sweating. I wiped my forehead and dried my palms on my pants.

I'd almost forgotten what had woken me, until I heard more yelling coming from downstairs. I stepped toward my door, the floor creaking under my weight, and I peeked around the corner. The hallway was long, dark, and empty. I tiptoed closer, listening to Mother and Father. I hated walking around without socks on. Sometimes, our wood floors gave me splinters in my toes. As I sneaked toward my parents, I walked carefully. Jagged pieces of wood in our floors were like God. I couldn't see them, but I knew they were there. And sometimes, they'd make their presence known. God did that by speaking through the pastor, telling me what he wanted me to do, and the wood spoke through splinters nestled so deeply that Father had to cut my skin just to get them out.

"This is absolutely unacceptable."

I crouched down on the top step, listening.

"Darling, please calm down," Father said. His voice was soothing, and it made me sleepy. I could fall asleep anywhere while listening to his stories of the other world. I loved when he told me about the day he met Mother. He'd said she was the most beautiful woman he'd ever met. He'd known from the moment he saw her that he wanted to be hers. He'd told me he hoped I'd someday find the love of my life, too. Thankfully, I didn't have to wait as long as he did, because God had brought me Abi already.

"I certainly will not calm down! We're talking about an arranged marriage for our son—our *preteen* son!"

I wanted to see more, so I tiptoed down another step, leaning forward until I could sneak a peek without being seen.

"I'll admit, it is a bit unorthodox, but this could be a good way to bring the community together under new leadership." Father stepped closer to Mother, pulling her into a hug. He wrapped his arms around her, holding her tightly. She tried pushing away, but he wouldn't release her. "Wouldn't it be nice to step back and focus on ourselves? We've always talked about having another baby."

I gasped at that. Another baby? I wanted a brother so badly. I'd asked for one for Christmas one year, but God never brought me one. This year, God brought me Abi, and now He might bring me a baby brother? I could barely contain my excitement. I wanted to clap and jump up and down and shout for joy, but I didn't, because Mother said it wasn't polite to eavesdrop.

"If you could just hear yourself..." She shook her head.

"I do, and yes, marrying off our son to grow our family isn't normally something I'd consider, but the pastor made some good points. We're talking about a marriage here, not sex. No one is expecting Abigail to bear a child."

Mother scoffed, finally breaking free of Father's embrace. "Don't be ridiculous." She waved away his concern. "He's a *child*. He needs to do childlike things, like go to school, play outside, *grow up*."

"He will also be the leader of this community one day, dear. That entails certain...responsibilities. If the pastor is willing to unite Abigail and James for the better of the community, I don't see why we shouldn't support it."

"Because we're talking about marrying off our only son! He's not even a teenager yet. *That's* why we shouldn't support it!"

Mother's face was red, and her arms were waving frantically as she yelled at Father. I didn't understand why they were fighting. If God wanted me to marry Abi, then I would marry her. Mother always told me to respect and obey my elders. I didn't understand why she was upset now.

Father exhaled slowly, running a hand through his hair. "I'll admit that I wouldn't have chosen this as a way to unite the community or as a way to make us stronger, but what other choice do we have here?"

"We could say no."

"But is that the best decision or is that a selfish one? We want to say no because of James, because we want him to enjoy his childhood. Is that not selfish of us? Shouldn't we think of the community?"

Mother shrugged. "I think it's a bit selfish of the community to ask us to marry off our only child."

"Perhaps it is, but when we started Living Light, we

knew we'd be asked to make tough decisions in order to bring together a group of strangers."

"This just..." Mother wrapped her arms around her chest. "This just can't be the right way." She spoke softly, calmly, and Father reached for her, tucking a loose strand of hair behind her ear.

After a few minutes of silence, I tiptoed back to bed. With thoughts of marriage and arguments in my mind, I drifted to sleep, unsure of what tomorrow would bring.

CHAPTER NINE

By the time I'd decided walking from Brooklyn to Manhattan was a ridiculous idea, I was already late for dinner. I thanked the taxi driver and exited the car, nearly forgetting the bundle of roses I'd stopped to get on my way home. I took the steps to our apartment two at a time until I reached the door. Inside, I found Jezebel busily cleaning the kitchen, two plates of food sitting atop the breakfast bar countertop.

"I'm so sorry, babe," I said as I approached her.

She exhaled slowly as she turned to face me, her eyes widening at the sight of the two dozen roses I'd picked up. "They're beautiful," she said as I handed them to her. She closed her eyes, inhaling dramatically, her nose mere centimeters from a blossoming bud.

"I'm sorry I'm late. I know this was an important night," I said, hoping she wouldn't press me about my whereabouts.

"I was worried," she said. Only then did I notice her worry wrinkles, as if she'd been frowning for the past several hours. Her hair was tied back, but loose strands from a busy day spilled from the clip. The heat had frizzed the hair around her ears, and she nervously tugged the loose strands into place as I stared at her.

"I know. I'm sorry I didn't text you."

She grabbed a glass vase from the cabinet, filled it with water, and placed the roses in it. "What kept you?" she asked as she rearranged each stem.

I could tell she feared the worst. I'd never given her any reason to doubt my loyalty to her, but that was only because she didn't know the whole story. If I was honest, there was another girl. I didn't care for Abigail the way I cared for Jezebel, but that didn't make lying any less wrong.

Thankful she wasn't looking at me, I said, "I was with a potential client."

She nodded. "Business seems to be picking up. I'm glad."

"Dinner smells delicious," I said, hoping to change the subject.

"It's cold," she said softly.

I closed the space between us, wrapping my arms around her waist and pulling her close to me. "I'm sorry, Jezebel. It won't happen again. I promise."

She shrugged. "It's okay. You were working. I get it. I get carried away when writing sometimes." She turned in my arms and placed a soft kiss to my lips.

"Why don't you sit down? I'll reheat dinner," I said as I reached for a bottle of wine. I poured her a generous splash and watched as she retreated to the living room, plopping down on the couch in front of the television.

After a few minutes of radiated heat, I joined her. She smiled as I offered her a plate. With frizzy hair, no makeup, and wearing yoga capris and a tank top, she was beautiful. I was constantly amazed by how her simplest looks could leave me breathless. I leaned in and kissed her before sitting back and devouring my plate of chicken alfredo, only then realizing just how hungry I actually was.

"So," Jezebel said, setting her plate of half-eaten pasta on the coffee table, "Tara sold the film rights, and she's throwing me a party this weekend. All kinds of important people will be there. I'm stoked!" She squealed, clapping with excitement. And with that, my confident girl had returned.

I nearly choked on the pieces of chicken I'd been chewing. I swallowed down a gulp of wine.

Jezebel laughed, reaching forward and rubbing my back. "Are you okay?"

I nodded and set down my plate beside hers. "That's amazing news!"

"I know. I can't believe someone bought the film rights already. I mean, the book hasn't even been released yet. Do you know how rare of a deal that is?" she asked.

"I can imagine, but I'm not surprised. You're a terrific writer."

She blushed, and I felt the heat of her cheeks in my pants. I shifted, turning toward her.

"I mean it, and I'm only slightly disappointed that we don't have champagne in these glasses."

"Well, I know a fantastic way to celebrate that doesn't involve any alcohol," she said, wiggling her brows.

Before I could respond, she was straddling my lap, pressing her lips to mine. I grabbed the meaty flesh of her ass, squeezing it as she ground against me. I was already hard. It was as if my dick was in a perpetual state of readiness when she was in the room, and I was eager to abide by its rules.

She had my cock springing free of my pants before I even realized what was happening.

"I love that I make you hard without really trying," she said as she stopped kissing my lips so she could kiss my neck.

Secretly, I loved it when she kissed me there. Each flick of her tongue, nip of her teeth, and suck of her lips sent shock waves straight to my dick. And now, as she put in her best work yet, thunderbolts were striking my cock in full force.

I groaned as she rolled her hips, rubbing herself against me. I could come without her ever really touching me. That's how badly I wanted her. I think she knew that, too, and I think she secretly got off on the control she had over me, even if she was the one submitting.

She worked the buttons of my shirt and pulled it off. I leaned forward so she could pull off my undershirt. Exposed, I leaned back as she peppered kisses on my chest. She teased my nipple, playfully flicking it with her tongue, and I sucked my lip into my mouth. I was sure I didn't feel what she felt when I sucked her nipples, but even so, it was erotic as fuck, and it made me hornier than ever.

Only then did I realize I was the only one naked.

"I think we need to do something about your clothes," I teased.

She laughed. "Yeah? Should I strip for you, baby?"

I groaned. "Fuck, you're sexy as hell."

She stood, turned, and ever so slowly removed her yoga pants. She swayed back and forth until they fell to the ground.

I grasped my cock, slowly stroking it as I watched her.

She danced to music only she could hear as she pulled her tank top over her head. In only panties, she pulled the hair tie from her hair, letting her long, dark locks fall to her back.

I stroked my dick faster as my pulse quickened.

Running her hands through her hair, she bunched the loose strands, baring her back to me as she spun on her heels to face me. With still-swaying hips, she kept her eyes closed, and her breasts were full, soft, and staring at me. Her nipples were delicious hard peaks that I ached to taste.

She released her hair, running a hand down her soft curves until she reached her panties. Playing with the edge of the lace, she teased me, lowering them just enough to reveal the arch of her bare mound. She turned again, this time leaning forward, and slowly shook her ass in circles.

I increased the pressure on my dick, rubbing the pre-come over the head. I groaned as I squeezed it, wishing I was about to come because I was sinking inside Jezebel instead of sinking into my fisted hand.

The lower half of her meaty ass was exposed in the panties she wore, but even though I'd already seen it, I was no less excited when she finally removed them. At a painfully slow pace, she slid off her panties and let them fall to the floor. Kicking them to the side, she faced me.

I was breathing heavily as I stared at her naked body. I scanned every curve, every scar, every beautiful part of her. She watched me stroke my dick while I stared at her, knowing it was her teasing and her gorgeous body that brought me to the edge. My breath hitched. I was about to come.

Jezebel fell to her knees and slid my throbbing cock into her mouth. The difference was jarring. My hands were rough; her mouth was soft, wet, hot, welcoming. And it took only one hard suck for me to reach my climax.

I cursed as I came. Jezebel stroked the base of my dick with her hand, milking every last drop. She swallowed everything I released, pumping my dick, sucking on my sensitive tip.

I rolled my head back and closed my eyes. "Fuck. So good," I whispered.

I didn't feel her mount me until I was already sliding

inside her.

"Christ, Jezebel."

My dick was still hard, still eager to fuck her until she orgasmed, but I was sensitive. And her pussy, so fucking tight, was desperate to make me come again. I curled my toes as she bounced up and down on my cock. Her breasts bobbled in front of me, so I leaned forward and seized a nipple with my lips. I playfully nibbled on the hard bud before soothing away the sting with my flattened tongue.

I angled my hips until I was rubbing against the smooth spot deep inside her.

"Yes, fuck. Right there."

Her eyes were closed, and I knew she was close. I grabbed her hips, letting her rest while I took control. Sweat beaded my forehead as I thrust into her again and again. She gripped my shoulders, digging her nails into my flesh.

"I'm coming. I'm coming!" she cried.

She clenched down on my cock, a vise grip so tight I couldn't suppress my desire to come again. I orgasmed with her, shooting what I could muster deep within her core. My cock twitched, unable to come again, and I slowed my thrusts until we were both unmoving, breathless on the couch. She leaned against me, her nipples, still hard, rubbing against my skin, and her hair, damp with exhaustion, tickling my nose as I kissed her temple.

Jezebel moaned as she snuggled against me. "That was amazing." Her voice was low as she mumbled, drowsiness clearly taking effect.

"I couldn't agree more," I said.

My arms were wrapped around her, and I traced circles on her skin with my thumb. She shivered under my touch.

Before I could lean down to kiss her, a buzzing erupted in the silent apartment. Jezebel groaned, slid off me, and sprinted to where her cell phone lay on the kitchen countertop.

"Hello?" A few seconds passed as I watched her, unable to look away from the bare, heart-shaped ass that stared back at me. "Hello?" She sounded annoyed now. She ended the call, bringing the phone with her as she returned to me on the couch.

"Who was it?" I asked, knowing it was a stupid question. Obviously no one had answered her.

"I don't know. I've been getting a lot of hang-up calls lately, and sometimes I can hear someone breathing, but they don't answer me. I thought it was a prank, but now, I..." She shook her head and shivered.

I leaned over, pulled the blanket from beneath me, and covered her with it. "How long has this been happening?" I asked, unable to hide my annoyance.

She shrugged. "A while."

I turned to face her. "A while? And you're just telling me now? Christ, Jezebel. I *am* your bodyguard. Don't you think this is something I should be aware of?"

"I-I don't know. I thought it was no big deal. I—"

"But it could be a very big deal. I need to know these things. I can't protect you when you hide shit from me!"

I was angry, justifiably so. When Jezebel was taken, I was supposed to be protecting her, not indulging in a life I thought we couldn't have. Instead of escorting her, I let the idea of being together get the best of me. I put aside my bodyguard duties and relaxed. That was when Miller made his move. I would never make that mistake again.

I knew who had been calling Jezebel. Even though I was

sure Abigail was harmless, I was pissed that she was doing this. Abigail wasn't an idiot; she knew she was poking a sleeping lion. And I would stop at nothing to ensure Jezebel—and her recovery—remained protected.

"Why are you so angry with me?" she asked. Like me, she wasn't hiding her annoyance either.

I exhaled slowly. Fighting with Jezebel would get me nowhere. I'd been lying to her, so she didn't know the danger she could be in. I couldn't expect her to tell me about a few hang-up calls when she didn't know she very likely had another stalker on the loose.

"I'm sorry. I don't mean to be a dick right now. I just... I just worry about you. Work's been stressful, and I'm taking it out on you. I'm sorry."

"It's fine."

Her response was short, to the point, and anything but fine. She didn't know to be fearful, because I hadn't told her about Abigail's stalking tendencies. I could admit the truth now, but that would only lead to questions I still couldn't answer.

I had to admit, Abigail was playing a good game. She was calling from a blocked number, and even if Reynolds could trace it, it would probably only lead to a burner phone using any number of towers in Manhattan, telling us nothing new.

Abigail was no longer poking a sleeping lion. The lion was awake, hungry, and ready to make her his meal.

CHAPTER TEN

The summer heat was slick on my skin. I wiped away the sweat with the back of my hand, praying to God for the strength to make it through this sermon without passing out. I loved summer because we could have our church services outside. But summer in upstate New York was humid. Sometimes, it hurt to breathe. It felt like a hot, wet blanket was wrapped around my head, smothering my mouth and nose. I wasn't sure how many more days like this I could handle without a trip to our lake.

I scanned the group. Everyone was here. It was against the rules not to attend sermon. Even when sick, God expected you to show up, and so did the new pastor. I didn't know what he'd do if the sick didn't attend, and I figured everyone was too scared to ask. I didn't worry much because I was never sick. But I did want to ask why God was so strict with us ever since He sent the pastor here. In every sermon, the pastor seemed angry with us for something else we'd done that he didn't like. It was as if we couldn't ever please him. That was the first thing on my list of reasons why I didn't like him.

I hadn't been listening to him, and I felt guilty. I knew God would want me to pay attention. So would Mother and Father. I glanced over at them. They sat beside me, Mother holding

Father's hand as they listened to the pastor preach God's word. I sneaked a peek at Abi. She was sitting beside her father. Her ankles were crossed, and she sat up stick straight. I adjusted in my seat, matching her stance. She smiled when our gazes met, but her smile never reached her eyes. I wasn't sure why, but she always looked sad.

I looked past her and stared at the weeper. The breeze made the long branches blow in waves, and it reminded me of the water. I wiped the sweat at my forehead again and closed my eyes, but only for a moment.

"James," the pastor called. It was amazing how quickly a single-syllable word could terrify me. It was my name, and I heard it dozens of times every single day. But sometimes, on days like today, it could shoot an arrow straight to my gut, leaving me gasping for breath as my sputtering heart gave out.

My gaze flickered to his, and I offered a wide, but fake, smile. Had he just caught me dozing off? Had he heard my plea to take this sermon to the lake, where we could bask in God's land while floating adrift?

"Please stand," he said.

I obeyed without hesitation. Was he going to tell everyone I'd nearly dozed off in the heat? Sometimes, I thought he was a mind reader. He always seemed to answer my thoughts. It was creepy, and it was the second thing on my list of reasons why I didn't like him. I was making up my list as I spent more time with Abi and him, but these were perfectly good reasons to dislike someone, I thought. I wondered if he knew I didn't like him.

"It is my greatest honor to announce the engagement of James Blakely and my daughter, Abigail." Almost as if on cue, Abigail stood and curtsied, giving her audience a wide smile.

I scanned the group. Most seemed horrified, their faces contorted into shocked gasps. Those without furrowed brows clapped, but beneath their smiles and congratulations, I noticed something more sinister. Did they also doubt God's request that I marry Abi?

I looked back at Abi. She still stood, her knee-length pale-blue dress fluttering in the wind. Her hair was pulled back, showcasing her freckled nose and cheeks. I smiled when she looked at me. I tried to see something else in her eyes. Did she harbor similar feelings? Was her smile a lie, too?

I felt like I couldn't believe anyone anymore. Everyone said they were happy, but their happiness ended there. It never reached their smiles, their eyes, their actions. Was I the only one willing to follow God's plan?

I didn't understand everyone's shock. I didn't understand how marrying Abi would make our lives any different. Mother and Father were married, and they lived in the same house. I thought all that would change is that Abi would move into our house. We had another bedroom. It was small, but I thought Abi would like it.

When I told Father we should build a bookshelf for Abi to store her things when she moved into our house after we were married, he told me to hush and sent me to my room. Mother overheard, and she didn't speak the rest of the night.

The pastor explained that the wedding was scheduled for my sixteenth birthday, but I didn't really listen. Instead, I was watching my parents. They were sitting beside me, smiling. They nodded when the pastor spoke and laughed when he said something funny, but they seemed...different. They didn't look happy. Did they not want me to get married either?

After the sermon ended, the pastor insisted I walk Abi

back home. In silence, I led her to their house, with my parents just feet behind us. When I glanced back to make sure they were still there, I found them speaking quietly to our neighbor, Bobby's mom. Mother's skin was bright red as she frantically spoke. She looked angry, but her complaints were silenced by Abi's voice and the wind.

"I saw you sleeping," Abi said, smiling.

"I didn't sleep," I said, crossing my arms over my chest. I was defensive. What if she told the pastor? He would punish me. I didn't want to be whipped by his belt.

"Your eyes were closed," she countered.

"Only for a minute!"

"Did you not like the service?" she asked.

I shrugged. "It was too hot."

She nodded and grabbed her skirt, splaying it out around her. "I love that girls can wear dresses. It's cooler."

"I think we should have sermon at the lake. Then we can all be cool because we'll be in the water in our swimming suits!"

Abi and I laughed as I backstroked the rest of the way home. Thankfully, it was a short walk, because my arms hurt by the time I reached her stoop.

"Can you play later?" I asked.

"Come on, James. We need to go home," Father said before Abi could answer.

I frowned. "Maybe tomorrow." I skipped to my parents, waving over my shoulder to Abi.

Abi's house was only a short walk to my own, but it felt longer. My parents didn't speak, even when I asked to play outside after dinner. By the time we returned home, the silence was so loud I could hear my heartbeat in my head.

Before I took the stairs to my room, I asked, "Are you

angry with me for marrying Abi?"

Mother smiled. "Of course not, sweetheart." She brushed my overlong hair from my eyes.

"We're proud of you, James, and we're humbled by your devotion to God," Father added.

I smiled, but as I turned away, I noticed an odd exchange between my parents. There was something they weren't telling me.

CHAPTER ELEVEN

Now

I was sure the smell of fried bacon would wake Jezebel, but if it did, she pretended to be asleep. I was able to cook scrambled eggs, fry bacon, dice fruit, assemble a bed tray of flowers and freshly squeezed orange juice, and clean up the mess I'd made in the kitchen before she even opened her eyes. When I returned to the bedroom, tray in hand, I found her curled in a ball, the morning light shining on her face. I sat beside her, rested the tray on her bedside table, and tucked loose hair behind her ear. She shifted before our gazes met.

"Morning, beautiful," I said.

She smiled and stretched. Her nose crinkled, and she followed the scent back to the tray beside her. "Did you make me breakfast in bed?"

I nodded. "Eggs, bacon, OJ, and the paper on your tablet. What more could a girl ask for?" I winked.

"Well, I can think of a few things..." She trapped her lower lip between her teeth. Its descent back to normality was torturously slow and oddly erotic.

"You, my love, are insatiable." I leaned down and brushed my lips against hers.

"Only for you," she whispered.

She adjusted, sitting up and leaning against the gray,

tufted headboard. The white sheets were crisp and tangled around her feet. As she smoothed her bed head, I maneuvered the tray to rest on her lap, and she wasted no time devouring what I'd placed before her. I chuckled and returned to my side of the bed.

"Babe?" I said as Jezebel crunched on a piece of bacon— extra crispy, just the way she liked it.

"Hmm?" She didn't look at me as she busily ate her breakfast.

"I'm sorry. I know I've been acting like a dick lately. I don't mean to be," I said.

She nodded. "I know. I wouldn't exactly say *dick*, but sometimes, things have seemed...different." She swallowed a gulp of orange juice.

"I'm not used to this. I've been alone all my life, and I haven't had to answer to anyone since I left the military."

"I know. I get it. Really. It's okay." She used her fork to play with her eggs, pushing them around until she scooped a bite into her mouth.

I ran my hand over her bare arm. "Do you know how incredible you are?" I asked her.

She snorted, and I continued.

"Don't believe for even a second that I don't know how lucky I am to be with you."

She glanced at me, leaned over, and ran her thumb along my jawline. "I'm pretty lucky, too," she whispered.

"I don't know what I'd do without you," I said, turning my head to kiss her thumb.

I knew what this would mean to her. When she was taken, she was hung by her arms. The restraints were so tight that her hands lost almost all blood. By the time I found her and we were taken to the hospital, the doctors needed to remove the skin that was beyond repair. Because of this, small chunks of her fingertip flesh were gone.

While I'd argue it wasn't noticeable unless it was something you looked for, Jezebel felt differently about it. For months after we returned home, I'd find her staring at herself in a mirror. She was gaunt from lying in a coma. She was scarred from the abuse she'd suffered. Her body was frail, limp. Every day I reminded her how beautiful she was, because even though her outer appearance had changed, she was still the most beautiful soul I'd ever seen.

I stood and winked. "When you're done, join me."

"Join you where?" she asked.

I didn't respond. Instead, I pulled my shirt over my head and yanked down my shorts. I chuckled as she gasped, and I could feel her gaze trailing the length of my nude frame, likely settling on my bare ass. I left my clothes in a pile on the floor and walked into the bathroom. Turning on the faucet, I adjusted the temperature so I wouldn't scald us when we climbed in.

The floor squeaked as she approached. Already nude, she smiled as she stood on her tiptoes to kiss me. She parted her lips, and our tongues met. She tasted like oranges. I smacked her ass while fucking her mouth with my tongue. She squeaked, and I grabbed her, lifting her so I could carry her into the shower. Her long legs wrapped around me, her heels lodging in the indent of my lower back.

She closed the shower door behind us, laughing as the water dowsed her. She pushed her hair from her eyes as I grabbed her bottle of shampoo. Plopping a pea-sized amount onto my palm, I reached for her hair.

"You're kidding, right?" She looked from my eyes to my

palm and back again.

"This is all I use."

"Well, you don't have all this," she said, pointing to her head. She turned, offering me a perfect view of her ass.

"You're right. I don't have nearly as tight of an ass as you do." I spanked her again, and she spun around, giggling.

"Not cool, and gimme that," she said, grabbing the bottle of shampoo and dumping at least ten times the amount of shampoo I'd put on my palm.

"Christ, Jez. No wonder you go through a bottle a week."

She laughed but turned toward the showerhead. I lathered the shampoo in my hands, careful not to drop any, and massaged her head. She moaned approvingly as I worked her temples.

"Keep your eyes closed," I said. She nodded. "And don't move." I laughed as I wiped the soap from her forehead before it slid too close to her eyes.

I ran my fingers through her tresses, lathering each strand from root to tip. Bunching her length in my palms, I brought her hair to her scalp and massaged her again. She rested her palms against the shower wall, rubbing her ass against my erection.

"That feels amazing," she said.

"My dick in your ass or my fingers in your hair?" I asked, smiling.

She thought for a moment. "Both."

I released her so she could rinse, smacking her ass once again. I left a bright-red handprint on her pale skin.

"You're making me wet," she said as she rinsed.

Suds dripped down her body until the water ran clear. Watching her rinse the soap from her hair was oddly erotic, and I couldn't wait to see it again. I grabbed her body wash, squeezing a generous amount onto my hand before returning the bottle to the shelf. I lathered the vanilla-scented wash over her breasts before moving on to the rest of her body. She turned so I could wash her back. I did so quickly because I was more interested in *other* areas.

She pulled her hair to the side, offering me access to her neck. As I wrapped my arms around her to wash her stomach, I kissed her neck. She moaned approvingly, arching her back to rub her ass against my hardened length. I bit her neck as I ran my hand over her mound. She gasped as I slid a finger between her lips.

I rubbed her clit with one hand and her breasts with the other. I twisted her nipples between the pads of my fingers until they were hard peaks. She moaned approvingly, so I continued my assault. I sank my finger into her depths. I pumped into her—once, twice. I pulled out and then shoved two fingers in. I stretched her, reveling in the fact that my dick actually fit inside this tight pussy.

"You're going to make me come," she said.

"That's the idea," I said, grinning against her neck.

I bit into the skin there, and she gasped. I dragged my teeth against her tenderness before sucking, licking, kissing away the sting of my mark.

Angling my hips, I slid inside her. My ascent was slow as I took her inch by inch. I spread her cheeks, watching as I disappeared inside. Watching myself fuck Jezebel was the sexiest thing I'd ever seen. I loved seeing how her body reacted to mine. She was always ready, always so fucking wet for me.

I slipped inside her easily, her pussy giving way to my girth. She was wet. Her cunt begged for more as I continued sinking deeply into her, inch by inch.

Jezebel wasn't known for her patience, and she quickly slammed her ass against me. My dick rubbed against her farthest depths as I entered her.

"Christ," I whispered.

My cock ached to release, but I wasn't ready yet. I curled my toes as I thrust into her, hard, fast, deep. I reached around and grabbed her breast. I squeezed her nipple and felt her pussy clench around my dick approvingly.

"Harder," she moaned.

I lifted her hips so she had to stand on her tiptoes. The water showered down on us, turning the pale skin of her back a bright red. I hadn't realized the water was so hot.

"Yes, fuck. Right there," she moaned.

My abs ached, but I wouldn't relent. Not until Jezebel reached her climax. I waited for her. Always. There was no feeling comparable to her orgasming because of how I made her feel.

"Come with me," I said, my voice deep, almost painful as I clung to my impending orgasm.

"Now. Right now," she said.

She grasped my dick, her pussy clenching me so hard I nearly passed out. I leaned against her, shooting my essence inside her until the final twitches of my cock were almost painful.

Pulling out, I watched as my come leaked down her leg and pooled between her feet.

"At least we don't have to clean up," she said, laughing.

CHAPTER TWELVE

N o w

Jezebel was scrolling through her phone, looking for a new takeout restaurant we hadn't tried for tonight's dinner, when a sudden, sharp knock erupted in the apartment. She jolted upright, gaze darting to the front door. She swallowed hard, her knuckles whitening as she gripped her phone.

My hand was on her knee, and I squeezed it reassuringly, offering a small smile before I rose to answer the door. I peeked through the hole, and saw two men, one young and one older, both in suits, standing outside the door. Every nerve ending in my body was aflame. These guys were definitely cops. Undoubtedly they were here because of something Abigail had done. Why else would the cops be here? I didn't believe in coincidences. My days of lying to Jezebel and covering up the truth were over. How was I going to explain that I'd been lying to her for days now?

"James? Who is it?" Jezebel asked.

"Cops," I said as I opened the door against my better judgment.

I nodded at the two men, watching as the younger assessed me. I was taller and more muscular than most men. I knew my appearance could be intimidating. Maybe that would work to my advantage here. I was skilled in interrogation techniques.

Surely I could counter anything Abigail had said.

"Can I help you?" I asked.

"I'm Detective Montemurro. This is my partner, Detective Price. Are you Mr. James Blakely?" the older of the two asked. He was shorter than me but still tall, with tanned skin and short-cropped salt-and-pepper hair. His partner, on the other hand, was frail in comparison. He was short, maybe only a few inches taller than Jezebel, his slender frame juxtaposed against his cocky grin and buzzed hair. Clearly he was trying much too hard to look like a badass.

I arched a brow. "Yes. I'm James Blakely."

"We'd like to speak with you. Do you have a few minutes now? If not, we can schedule something at our precinct for later."

I grinned. Of course he was hoping I'd ask to speak later. He was counting on me not to be prepared for such a visit, but I'd expected Abigail to do something reckless. Even so, I wasn't sure Jezebel was prepared for this moment.

I glanced back to find her rising from the couch to meet me at the door. I exhaled slowly. It was now or never. If they took me to the precinct, she'd have questions. I couldn't lie to her about their intentions. But if we were to do this at home, I could spend the next several hours—or maybe the rest of my remaining years—begging her to forgive me for lying to her about Abigail.

"Now is fine," I said.

I stepped aside, and the two men walked into the apartment. I watched as they scanned their new surroundings, ensuring the area was safe for them both. Price's gaze lingered far too long on Jezebel, traveling the length of her. Though it irked me, I couldn't blame him. She was gorgeous. With pale skin, dark hair, pouty lips, and a curvy body, she was both exotic and erotic. My two favorite things.

"Hi. Jezebel Tate." She offered her hand, and both men returned her handshakes. "Would you like something to drink?"

"No, ma'am. Thank you," Montemurro answered. Price had yet to speak. I wondered if that was his *thing*. After all, he was trying to act tough.

She nodded and crossed her arms over her chest, visibly uncomfortable that Price had yet to look away from her.

"So, what's this about?" I asked, annoyed. I walked to Jezebel's side, half blocking Price's view. He was close enough for me to look down at him, and I was sure he got the message.

"Mr. Blakely, I'm sorry to be the one to tell you this, but your parents' remains were found in upstate New York."

My breath caught. My heart was pounding so hard, I could feel it in my head, the rushing noise almost unbearable. Anger boiled in the pit of my gut. Were they seriously talking about this in front of Jezebel? They didn't think this might be too personal of an announcement? They couldn't ask me to speak with them alone? What the fuck was I going to say now? She knew I'd been acting strangely ever since the news report. She'd know I've been keeping this from her. When she learned I'd also been lying about a certain redhead, she'd never forgive me.

Jezebel gasped beside me. Her delicate hands covered the shock on her face, but I was sure her jaw was smacking the ground just as mine was—though for different reasons.

"We're so very sorry for your loss, Mr. Blakely," Montemurro said.

"Oh my God, James," Jezebel whispered beside me. She

closed the short distance between us, slinging her arm around my waist. She pulled me close to her, and I could feel everyone's eyes on me. It was an odd feeling, a sense I'd developed while overseas.

The military put me in dangerous situations, and it was my job to watch my back and the backs of my brothers. Honing this skill was something I used to be proud of. Now, I hated the feeling. It was like shards of glass slicing my eyelids open. I could feel their stares, judging me, pitying me, waiting for me to respond.

Again, what the fuck was I supposed to say?

Yeah, my parents are dead. I know that. I killed them.

Jezebel sucked in a sharp breath.

Had I just said that aloud?

"Mr. Blakely? Are you okay?" Montemurro asked.

He took a small step toward me, and I wanted to push him away. I wanted to push him out the door and toss Price out right behind him. I couldn't handle this right now. I had to keep Jezebel in the dark until I knew it was safe to bring her into the light. I had to find Abigail before she told the world what really happened. I had to keep the identity of my parents under wraps, which I was already failing at miserably. I didn't have time to be scrutinized over my reaction to the death of my parents. I'd swallowed that sword long ago. I didn't want to relive it now.

I nodded but said nothing. Jezebel's grip on my arm was painful. She was trying to be comforting, but this entire situation was smothering me.

"There was evidence of a...community living there. We're here as a courtesy to our friends up north. It's not our jurisdiction, but they wanted us to assure you that they are doing everything they can to scout the area and find out what happened to your parents."

I groaned internally. A high-scale investigation into my past was exactly what I didn't need right now.

"How do you know they're my parents?" I asked, finally speaking.

"As a service member, your DNA was in the system. When we find a body, we run its DNA against everything we can. This includes the military database."

I nodded. Apparently I'd put myself in this situation. I was shocked this wasn't part of Abigail's plan.

"Do you know anyone who'd want to harm your parents, Mr. Blakely?"

I shook my head. "I can't remember. I don't remember anything from that time. I was young, traumatized..." I'd already said too much. I should have stopped at young. Better yet, I should have stopped at no. "I wish I could help you. I really do. Is there anything else?" I hoped I wasn't coming off as an emotionless sociopath.

"Here, let me give you my card." Montemurro reached into his suit jacket pocket and pulled out a crisp white business card. He handed it to me. "If you remember anything, anything at all, you can call me directly. My number is listed there."

I nodded and shoved the card into my pocket. "Thanks for doing this, for coming here, for...finding them."

"Well, we played no role in the discovery, but I'll pass along your gratitude when I speak with the head detective of that precinct."

So he was going to write a report on our meeting. Fan-fucking-tastic. Could this day get any worse?

"As a courtesy, Mr. Blakely, don't leave the city anytime

soon," he added.

Fuck my life. I nodded and assured him I had no plans to leave the area. Before they could ruin my day even more, I quickly escorted them out, slamming the door behind them a little harder than intended.

"Great," I mumbled under my breath.

"You lied," Jezebel said as soon as I turned around. "Why not tell them the truth? You're innocent in this crime, James."

"This is... It's just too much right now. You're the only person I've ever told."

When Jezebel had spilled her secrets to me about the death of her parents, in a moment of weakness, I'd opened up to her. I'd told her I'd lived in a self-sufficient community and that a man came and murdered everyone. But I'd never told her about Abigail, about our planned marriage, about how I'd left everything behind. I was embarrassed that I had been used as a tool to further his plan, and now, I was guilt-stricken for lying to her for so long.

"So no one else knows about what happened back then?"

Swallowing the knot that was truly beginning to suffocate me, I lied to the woman I loved. Again. "No. No one else knows."

CHAPTER THIRTEEN

THEN

A loud knock echoed through our small home. I ran to the door and found the pastor. I scowled, unable to control myself. I wanted to turn him away. I didn't like him, and I was sure my parents didn't like him. I'd considered asking him to let Abi move in here so she didn't have to be around him either.

"James," he said, nodding his head as he pushed past me into the hallway. "Where are your parents?"

I wanted to push him back. I didn't care if he was the pastor. He couldn't come into my home without permission. We had strict rules at Living Light. Mother once told me you had to lock up everything in the other world, but here, we didn't do that. We trusted our neighbors. I tried pushing him out the door, and he smirked. Anger boiled inside me.

Before I could answer his question and tell him to leave, Mother turned the corner, her smile fading when she saw the pastor.

"James, go to your room," she said. Her tone was short, her face in a scowl.

I frowned. Had I upset her? I'd been rude to the pastor, and Mother always told me to respect my elders. But he didn't deserve my respect. Was I supposed to respect someone undeserving? I didn't know what to say to relieve her anger, so

I said nothing.

"Now, James," she added.

I nodded and ran up the stairs, pretending to go to my room. When I reached the top step, I crouched down, hiding in the shadows. I knew it was disrespectful and against the rules to eavesdrop, but I also knew there were things my parents weren't telling me. If I didn't listen, how would I find out what they were hiding?

"You announced the marriage at the sermon. We never gave our official approval!" Mother said.

She was angry. Her hands were balled in fists at her sides. She frowned, her forehead wrinkling. I'd never seen Mother so angry. Maybe she wasn't upset with me. Maybe she was mad at the pastor. I couldn't help my smile. Maybe she would tell him to leave and never come back. He could leave Abi here. I would take care of her.

"I gave you a week to respond," he said simply.

I grimaced at his smugness. I didn't know why I hated him so much. It upset me that God used him. Why didn't He speak through someone else—someone more deserving? Father would be a good prophet. I sent a silent prayer to God, telling Him He should really reconsider speaking through the pastor. I made sure to speak nicely, because Mother once said we are never to question God.

Sometimes, I didn't believe the pastor even loved God. I knew it was a crazy thought, but I trusted my instincts. The only other time I hated someone right away was when I met Tommy. He and his parents moved here a few years ago, but they had to leave when Tommy wouldn't follow the rules. He would sneak into houses and steal things. He would skip sermon. He would fight other kids. My parents told him to behave, but he never did. I'd always hated Tommy.

"We've decided not to move forward with the marriage," Father said. I hadn't heard him enter the room, so I took a couple of steps toward them, hoping I could see better.

Father was taller than the pastor, so I knew when I grew up, I'd be taller than him, too. I think the pastor didn't much like my parents. Maybe he was scared of Father because he was a stronger man. I hoped I'd grow up to be stronger than the pastor, too. Father said it was my responsibility to care for the community because it would be mine someday. So when God told the pastor I was to marry Abi, I knew it must be true. Abi and I would lead the community together. I smiled at the thought.

"James is too young for this," Mother said.

Again, her tone was short, and she crossed her arms over her chest. She never spoke to me that way. I was happy I never upset her so much. I tried hard to follow the rules, so I didn't understand why the pastor could so easily break them and not get in trouble. Father always said there was an order. Before the pastor came, Father helped with sermon. But now, the pastor said he's not allowed.

"I mentioned that the marriage wasn't happening until they were sixteen," the pastor replied. Everything about the pastor seemed mean, from the way he spoke to you to the way he looked at you. Patiently, I waited for Mother to tell him he was no longer welcomed at Living Light.

"That's still too young," Mother countered. "We want him to grow up, to be a kid, to follow his passions. He can't do that married to your daughter."

Why was she explaining the same things over and over again? Why didn't she see what I saw? She needed to send him away. He didn't belong here.

"This marriage will solidify my role in this community. We need to maintain order." The pastor sounded angry, his voice gruff.

I balled my own fists, ready to charge the pastor if he hurt Mother. Father was there, but he hadn't spoken again.

"That's what this is about, isn't it? You want control of the community."

"I want the community to succeed in my vision, yes."

"In *your* vision?" Mother scoffed.

"I speak for God," he said simply. "And God would like you to join me in this cause."

I was so angry. I was upset with God for choosing to speak through the pastor. I was angry the pastor was so mean to us. But mostly, I felt bad for Abi. I didn't want her to live with him anymore.

"This is not happening, Pastor. Either you fix this, or we're taking James and leaving. And believe me, more will follow us."

CHAPTER FOURTEEN

Jezebel squeezed my hand as we stood just outside the small gallery. The front of the building consisted of wall-to-wall floor-to-ceiling windows. Inside, I could see paintings of modern art that closely resembled the art Jezebel painted at home. Each canvas was splashed with color, each stroke seemingly unintentional, but real care had gone into every mark. That was what I loved about modern art. It looked like a mess, but truthfully, it was organized.

As I took in the scene before me, I was baffled. Tara had accomplished the impossible. She'd secured a location in Manhattan for a last-minute weekend party. While I admired Tara's talent as a negotiator, Jezebel seemed tense beside me.

"This is the perfect place," I said, trying to ease her nerves. She nodded.

"Good crowd, too. Not too many people." I offered a wide smile.

Again, she nodded.

I cleared my throat. "Come on, love. Your minions await." This time, she chuckled. Score!

"There are more people than I was expecting. I can see the production company's team in there. What if they ask me how the writing's going and they hate my answer? What if they want me to kill off the main characters or something drastic?"

"You write romance, babe. They're businessmen. The number-one rule in the romance business has got to be not to kill off your protagonist or the love interest."

"Nicholas Sparks kills off his characters all the time."

"Yes, but he writes love stories. Love stories are tragic. You write romance. To quote a pretty fabulous writer I know, 'Romances are just wicked hot.'"

She rolled her eyes and playfully smacked my arm before leaning against me. I smiled as I reminisced about the time Jezebel told me that. We'd had a similar conversation after I'd finally read one of her books. I hadn't been prepared for its promiscuity, and she'd told me that romances are supposed to be wicked hot. Though her stalker was afoot, life seemed simpler then.

"This is pretty awesome, isn't it?" she asked.

She eyed the crowd inside, but I eyed her. Jezebel was the strongest person I'd ever known. I was often in awe of her strength. She'd overcome so much in her young life. I couldn't comprehend the moments she felt weak. I couldn't understand how she didn't see what I saw every time I looked at her—one hell of a strong woman.

"Yeah. Pretty awesome," I said.

Hand in hand, we emerged from the darkness of the street and entered the chaos of the party. The moment she stepped into the room, she was a star. I met more people that evening than I'd met over the few years I'd lived in Manhattan. To be honest, I couldn't remember anyone's name. Director this, producer that... All I cared to do was watch Jezebel in her element. There was truly nothing more beautiful than a creature in its natural habitat. She was fierce, wild, strong-willed, and utterly gorgeous. I was proud to be on her arm, to spend this night with her.

"We've contracted a couple different writers to work on the screenplay. We'd love for you to be part of the decision process for the final script," a man with light-blond hair said. He was young, and his pale-blue eyes sparkled when Jezebel looked at him.

Jezebel smiled. "I'd love to participate."

"Perfect. I can have Mary handle the details with Tara."

I leaned in, brushing loose hair behind Jezebel's ear. She shivered under my touch. A movement so brief, so simple, yet so intimate, I was sure no one but me witnessed it, even though all eyes were on Jezebel. "I'm going to get us some drinks." I placed a kiss to her temple, nodded to the man we'd been speaking to, and walked to the bar.

"Two glasses of champagne, sir?"

My cock stirred at the thought of the other night.

"Yes, please."

"Make it three," a familiar voice said. "I'm impressed. This doesn't seem like your scene. How did Jezebel convince you to attend?"

"There's nothing I wouldn't do for her, Tara. You know that."

She smiled, nodding. "You two are most definitely in that annoying lovey-dovey stage."

I didn't have the heart to tell her that this was definitely not a stage. Jezebel would bring me to my knees long after these beginning years.

"She looks gorgeous tonight," Tara said, eyeing Jezebel from across the room.

I followed her gaze, nodding my approval. "There's never

a moment when she doesn't," I said softly.

"She's really recovered well. I think we owe that to you, James," Tara said.

I shook my head. "It was all her. She wanted to see a therapist and put in the work to get better. I was just there to witness it."

Tara smiled. "You truly don't see it, do you?"

I arched a brow. "See what?"

"You're her anchor. You've been a blessing, James. A godsend."

I cringed at the thought. Ever since Living Light, I'd done my best to keep God out of my life.

"She was strong enough to face what happened, confront her past, because you were there, right beside her."

"As were you," I said.

She shook her head. "Not in the same way. You were able to help Jezebel love herself again. You showed her she was deserving of love. I couldn't do that for her, even as her best friend. I'd prayed someone would come into her life and make her see just how invaluable she is."

I swallowed hard and stared at Tara. I didn't know what to say. I couldn't take credit for the hard work Jezebel had put into her recovery, because all I did was be there when times were too tough for her to stand alone. In those moments, I carried her *and* her demons.

She smiled at me. "It's okay to admit you were an important part of her recovery."

Tara was a few years older than Jezebel. They'd both attended the same undergrad university, and since they'd both majored in English, they'd had a few classes together. It hadn't taken long for them to bond over books and lattes. I imagined them staying up late, confessing their love for the written word.

Aside from that, Tara was Jezebel's opposite in every sense of the word. She had dark-black skin and short, natural hair. She loved to work. Her business was put before anything else. She was technical, whereas Jezebel was emotional. Occasionally, Jezebel's inability to take the business side of this industry seriously annoyed Tara to no end, but she loved her like a little sister. I was grateful for Tara.

"If I'm taking credit here, then you should, too," I said.

"What'd I do?"

"Well, for one thing, you told her to hire a bodyguard. I literally can't thank you enough for introducing us."

She barked out a hard laugh.

"I think Jezebel admires you. She may not share your disdain for emotional thinking, but you are definitely the person she wants to be like when she grows up."

"Aw, James. You're a big softy!" She smacked my arm, smiling.

I laughed, but something just beyond her silhouette caught my eye. "Incoming," I said, turning as a stranger approached, her sights on Tara.

Instead, I set my sights on Jezebel, watching as she laughed at a joke someone made. Her eyes grew wide, her hand covered her mouth, and she bellowed loudly. I didn't regret missing the joke, but I did regret missing the way she'd lean against me when something was too funny for her to even hold her own weight. Without me there, she had to support herself. Once again, I was in awe of her strength. It wasn't too long ago she was fighting for her life. So few people experience what she went through and live to tell the story. But if anyone could do it, I wasn't surprised that it was my sexy wordsmith.

My eyes trailed her frame. She wore a form-fitting, dark-teal dress. It was sleeveless and low-cut, leaving her back nearly bare, especially with her hair pulled back. Her strappy black heels made her legs even longer. I ached to rip off her dress. I was sure she'd picked out this attire for just this occasion.

I didn't know much about fashion. Thankfully, men had it easy. Most days, I wore a suit, but even when I dressed casually, I noticed the approval simple jeans and a T-shirt received. I'd put effort into my look tonight, not wanting to disappoint her. I'd styled my hair, trimmed my "shadow," as Jezebel liked to call it, and even ironed my suit. At her request, I'd ditched the tie and left the top buttons of my shirt undone. I knew this look made her crazy, and I'd felt her lustful eyes on me all night.

Someone grabbed Jezebel's attention, so she said goodbye to the man who was monopolizing a bit too much of her time. I couldn't see the woman she was speaking with now, but I assumed she was some producer at the company. I wished I knew more about this industry, because sadly, I had nothing cunning to say when people asked about my role in the publishing world.

"Just tell people you're the man responsible for bringing everyone together," Jezebel had said when I brought this concern to her this morning. "I mean, it's your job to protect a pretty important piece."

"Sir?" someone said, bringing me back from my memory.

I turned toward the bartender. Tara was already happily sipping her drink. I added a twenty to the tip jar and took the two remaining glasses.

"It's a great party, Tara. Thanks for doing this," I said when she wasn't speaking with the brunette who'd sauntered over earlier.

She smiled. "Jez deserves this."

"Mrs. Johnson," I said to Tara, smiling and nodding as I turned to walk back toward Jezebel.

"It saddens me to know Jezebel will ruin one of the last remaining polite men with her brazen tendencies," Tara said as I walked away.

Internally, I chuckled. She was right. Jezebel was turning me into a sexual fiend, and I definitely didn't care.

"Champagne," I said, offering Jezebel her glass. She blushed as she took it, dragging her teeth over her lower lip. I suppressed a groan, even though my dick throbbed in response. She had a way of capturing my complete attention, and I was sure she knew of this power she had over me.

"Well, it was great meeting you, Miss Tate. Thanks so much for answering my questions."

Time slowed as the sound of that voice enveloped me. I was sure I'd remember it until the day I died. It haunted me in a way I could never escape. It reached for me, offering a firm grasp around my neck, suffocating me while I stood, shocked, silent, stationary. It hurt to breathe, to blink, to swallow. These moments were eerie and often left for the likes of horror films, not real life.

I watched as Jezebel's lips moved, but I heard nothing. I was stunned, paralyzed, terrified of seeing her so close to the woman I loved, to the woman who had no idea that my past was literally mere feet from her. The noose was tightening, and only when Jezebel spoke my name did I free myself from it.

"James? You okay?" She rested her hand atop my own, which had, shockingly, not dropped the glass I was holding. Suddenly, I desperately needed something stronger than champagne.

"Who was that?" I asked, still unmoving.

She shrugged as she sipped the bubbly pink liquid from her glass. "A journalist. She's publishing an article on me, I guess. She looked really familiar, though. Maybe I've met her at a signing?"

The world fell silent as I finally faced her. She'd already walked away, but in the distance, just before she crossed the galley's threshold, she turned, a devilish grin plastered on her face. Her nefarious glare spoke volumes in the moment of deafening silence when our gazes met.

CHAPTER FIFTEEN

N o w

I downed my champagne, slammed the glass onto a waiter's tray harder than intended, and offered a weak excuse to Jezebel. By the time I reached the door and ran down the street, Abigail was gone. Still, I walked a few blocks, frantically scanning the storefronts and alleyways, ignoring those who begged for money, their signs for help nothing but blurs.

When I reached the end of the block, I decided I'd never find her this way. She was baiting me, I was sure. I just needed to play her game, but I found it nearly impossible to think straight. I'd been searching for her for so long, and now she was right before me, taunting me with a powerful, yet risky, move. How had she known I hadn't told Jezebel all about her? How had she known she wasn't on some refusal list?

I gasped. The list! Tara had hired an amazing event coordinator to ensure tonight was successful, and the coordinator required everyone to flash an ID or ticket to get into the event. After all, this was an exclusive party. Only invitees could attend. So how had Abigail scored a pass?

I ran back to the gallery, my feet pounding the slick pavement. It must've rained while we were inside. I hadn't noticed. I was missing so many details lately that I was embarrassed to be looking for work as a bodyguard. Sure,

Jezebel didn't really need my expertise anymore. Miller was gone. But a new demon had entered this hell. Jezebel just didn't know that yet. Again, I'd let my guard down. I wasn't sure what it was about Jezebel that made me lose all control of my faculties when she was around.

I reached the gallery just as the sting in my chest was becoming annoying. I gasped for breath as I scanned the crowd. Jezebel was talking to Tara—probably about me. I couldn't worry about that now. I had to find the coordinator. I'd seen her when we arrived, but I hadn't paid much attention to her. Mentally, I retraced my steps to the party, trying to recall her face. She was young, but her hair was gray. An intentional dye job, I remembered thinking when I saw her.

"Can I help you find something, Mr. Blakely?" someone asked.

As if God Himself were listening—and for once, He was welcomed—the gray-haired beauty was staring back at me, a wide smile on her face. I was so happy, I could kiss those lips.

"Yes. There was a girl here today. She had long red hair, pale skin, blue eyes. Do you know who she is?"

Her brows wrinkled as she thought about my question. She shook her head. "I don't remember her name."

"But you remember her?" I asked.

"Oh, yes. I remember everyone's face. It's a curse, really."

"How did she get in without a pass?"

Her nose wrinkled now. "What do you mean?"

"She wasn't supposed to be here."

With wide eyes, she said, "But she had a pass." She scanned her list of names. "Yes. Yes! Here."

Abigail Martin. Press.

Martin. Her last name was Martin. I exhaled slowly, relief

washing over me. Knowing her last name would make my search for her much simpler. I prayed it wasn't fake.

"Yes, I remember now. She was with the press. She's writing an article on Miss Tate. She was really excited her request to attend was approved, because she was writing a story about Miss Tate, not about her book. She thought for sure she wouldn't be invited."

I ran a hand through my hair, my fingers tangling in the gelled strands. "She left." I spoke more for myself than for her.

The coordinator shook her head. "No, sir. She hasn't checked out yet."

"I watched her leave. She's gone."

"But...her coat," the girl turned slightly, pointing to a closed door. "You have to check out with me to get your belongings back. She must still be here."

For the first time in weeks, relief flooded over me. She'd wanted to be invited so she could leave me a clue. She wanted me to find her, which meant she knew I was looking for her. She was leaving breadcrumbs, hoping I was smart enough to find my way back to her.

"Show me her belongings."

The girl nodded and showed me into the small room. "That's it."

I grabbed the coat and started emptying the pockets.

"Umm... I should get back to the party."

I nodded without looking at her. I probably looked like a crazy person, but I was Jezebel's security. Ensuring her safety was my first priority. Sometimes, that meant riffling through someone's belongings and looking like I was having a psychotic break. For all I knew, I *was* having a breakdown. I made a mental note to have myself admitted after I stopped my past from destroying everything I've built.

All the pockets were empty save for one. In it, I found a crumpled business card of a private investigator. I ran a finger over the faded text. I didn't know many private investigators. When I needed someone found, I used my personal connections, but I wasn't surprised Abigail needed to hire such help. I shoved the card into my jacket pocket and hung the coat back on the hanger. I desperately wanted to go to the investigator now, but I'd already missed a good chunk of the party. Against my better judgment, I'd have to wait to pay him a visit until tomorrow.

I exited the storage area. The door slammed shut to the silent room. Jezebel had been making a speech, and now all eyes were on me. I'd missed it. I'd missed the party, the reading, the speech. And one look at Jezebel was a blade to the heart. She was crushed, and that look of despair, of regret, was there because of me.

CHAPTER SIXTEEN

Today's sermon was about forgiveness. The pastor explained that God would forgive our sins if we bared our truth to Him, and the pastor asked the community to forgive him of his.

I scanned the group, hoping no one would forgive him. Almost as soon as the feeling came, a sense of dread washed over me. I wasn't behaving the way God would want me to behave. I was angry, hateful toward the pastor—never giving him a true chance. I prayed that God would forgive my sins, and I promised I'd be nicer to the pastor. After all, God chose him for a reason, and I shouldn't doubt God.

Bobby smiled at me when our gazes met. I offered a small wave, hoping not to attract any attention. It was against the rules not to pay attention during the sermon. He made a funny face at me, and I covered my mouth with my hand to stop myself from laughing. His mom must've seen it, though, because she smacked the back of his head. He sat upright, gaze darting forward as he listened to the pastor give his sermon.

I glanced at my mom. She was watching the pastor, but she looked...different. I thought she was still angry with him. Maybe she would ask for God's forgiveness today, too. Everything would be okay. I reached for her hand, cupping it beneath my own. She glanced over and smiled.

Her eyes were the color of the sky. Father's eyes were the color of the grass. Once, I told them that was why God brought them together and told them to start Living Light. They laughed, but I saw something pass between them when they looked at each other again. I think they knew I was right about God's work. I wondered why they doubted His plan for Abi and me now.

The breeze picked up, blowing my hair from my eyes. It was a hot summer day, but I welcomed it. It was almost autumn. I loved how nature changed in autumn, but I hated the cold. Once, I'd asked my parents to move Living Light somewhere that was warm all year. That was how much I hated the cold.

I did like looking at the snow, though. I'd watch it fall through the windows. Fireplaces heated all of our houses during the winter, and Father had been working tirelessly all summer to gather enough wood for everyone. I glanced at him, wondering if I should help him chop wood after sermon instead of playing in the fields with Bobby.

My gaze shot to the pastor's the moment I heard my name.

"My loving daughter, Abigail, and James Blakely are no longer engaged to be married. I'll admit, my appreciation and admiration of the Blakely household stirred an excitement within me. I made the announcement without coming to a clear, beneficial decision for both our families and for the community. I am deeply sorry, and I do hope you all will forgive me for a rushed decision."

When the pastor met Mother's gaze, she smiled and nodded, but underneath, I could see it. She was no longer happy. I worried what that meant for our family and for Living Light. They'd said they'd leave, but would they really? I didn't want to leave. Living Light was all I knew. It was home.

"Mrs. Blakely," the pastor said. "Mr. Blakely."

"Pastor," Mother replied. Her voice sounded pleasant, but I knew she was faking it. I'd learned all of Mother's tics over the years. I always knew when she was upset, and today, she was hiding her anger.

"Again, I'd like to offer my sincerest apologies. I didn't handle the situation well. You were right; they are too young. Our focus should be on the current community, not on growing its future generation."

Mother snorted, rolling her eyes.

"Have you reconsidered my offer to stay? I'd hate to lose such prominent, resourceful members."

"No," Father said.

"We're leaving," Mother announced.

I gasped, as did several others. We were leaving? I glanced back and forth between Mother, Father, and the pastor. No one had told me we were leaving. I wanted to cry, to scream, to beg them to reconsider. I wondered if they doubted my ability to follow God's plan. I'd have to show them that I could do it. I could marry Abi. I could lead the community so they didn't have to anymore.

I gripped Mother's hand, and she squeezed mine in return. I knew that squeeze. It told me not to speak, not to make a scene. I swallowed my pain, my questions, and waited.

"May I ask why? I've called off the engagement. Is that not what you wanted?" the pastor asked. He looked hurt, as if his words pained him. His eyes were sad, but I wasn't sure if he was upset because Mother said we were leaving or because leaving meant I couldn't fulfill God's plan.

"Living Light was supposed to be a peaceful place, a refuge. That wasn't supposed to change after we relinquished leadership to you. You've turned it into...something else," Father said, finally speaking.

I glanced at him. He frowned, his lips pressed firmly together. I knew that look, too. He wanted this conversation to end. Father was a gentle man, so I didn't see it often. What was it about the pastor that brought out so much anger in our family? No one else seemed afflicted.

"Something we want no part of," Mother added.

The pastor nodded. "I do apologize. I didn't mean to make you feel like I ruined your life's work."

Mother brushed away his concern with the wave of her hand. I'd seen that many times, too. She was also done with this conversation, and if the pastor knew what was good for him, he'd leave her alone.

"We're leaving in a few days," Father said.

I gasped. In a few days? They'd already made plans? I'd hoped they'd only spoken in anger, but maybe they were serious. I couldn't shake the feeling that I didn't want to leave. I loved it here; I had friends and Abi. I didn't want to move somewhere else. I didn't want to leave Living Light.

CHAPTER SEVENTEEN

Now

The silence in the taxi ride back to the apartment was deafening. Jezebel wouldn't look at me, and when I reached for her hand, she pulled away. I understood she was furious with me. I'd been a terrible boyfriend. I'd lied, hidden my past, and broken my promises to her. If only she could understand that I was doing this to protect her. But she couldn't. Not until I came clean.

"It's the white one. Thank you," Jezebel said to our driver. He pulled over, and she opened her door, exiting without me. I paid the man and slammed the door. She was inside the building, so I took a moment to gather my thoughts.

The street was dark, the lights only illuminating small patches of the outside world. Bumper-to-bumper cars lined the street of historic homes. All were brownstones save ours. After Jezebel bought the top-floor apartment, a former tenant bribed the building manager to paint the brownstone white, and now, she affectionately refers to her home as a "whitestone."

Slowly, I took the stairs to the building and walked toward Jezebel, who was waiting for the elevator.

"My feet hurt," she said as an explanation for not taking the stairs, and I nodded. "Are you seriously giving *me* the silent treatment, Blakely? As if I'm in the wrong here!"

I cringed at her use of my last name. When we first met, she'd only ever called me by my last name. I knew it was her way of keeping me at a distance, and I welcomed it. I hadn't been in a rush to admit my feelings for her were deepening, and being referred to by my last name had kept our relationship physical, not emotional. But now, it stung.

"I can't believe you," she said, shaking her head. She pressed the call button again.

"I'm sorry."

"I know. You're always sorry. I just... What the hell is going on? What aren't you telling me?"

I exhaled slowly. "I can't, Jezebel. Please..."

"Does this have something to do with the detectives who showed up?"

I said nothing. I didn't want to lie. Not again.

"Talk to me!" she yelled. "Say *something*."

Her voice cracked, and I knew she was on the verge of crying. I couldn't handle knowing I'd made her break. For over a year, I was her rock. She'd come to me when the nights became too dark, the days too long. I'd held her while she cried herself to sleep more times than I could count. I'd begged her demons to take hold of me and release her. Eventually, they did.

"Just tell me what's going on," she said, a sob escaping her lips.

Again, I fell mute. I was ashamed, embarrassed by the role I'd played in the death of my parents, in the annihilation of my community. I'd been a pawn, and I'd played the part well. I couldn't admit that to her. I feared her reaction. I wouldn't let my past be the reason she looked at me differently. And I couldn't bear the thought of admitting I'd been lying to her this whole time.

The door to the elevator opened. I watched as she walked inside and pressed the button to her floor. My feet, suddenly anchored to the ground, didn't move.

Between hiccups, she said, "I don't understand why you aren't saying anything. Obviously you don't trust me." She pressed the button again.

"I have to protect you, Jezebel," I whispered.

She met my gaze. "This is about me? Then don't you think I have the right to know?"

I shook my head. I wasn't sure which question I was answering, but I was desperate for her to end this conversation. Almost as soon as I made my internal plea, someone answered my prayers. Was it God giving me an escape, or was it her demons, clinging to my soul just as soon as they released hers?

"Fine. Maybe you should get some space for a couple of days so you can figure this out since it's obviously more important to you than I am."

When the doors closed, I didn't stop them.

★ ★ ★

Almost as if I were truly a spineless droid, I found myself outside the private investigator's office. It was late, well past midnight, but a soft-yellow light illuminated a window. He could be in there. *She* could be in there. I fidgeted with the cuff of my jacket sleeve, stalling for time.

I should be back at the apartment, confessing my sins to Jezebel.

I should be getting some space away from this mess, maybe checking into a hotel to give Jezebel some time to rethink things.

I shouldn't be here. I shouldn't be thinking about Abigail. I shouldn't be standing outside, in the middle of the night, in the suit I wore to celebrate Jezebel's success, in Brooklyn's shadiest neighborhood, where garbage was piled high, the buildings needed fresh coats of paint, and a homeless man just defecated on the curb.

Mindlessly, I took the few steps to the front door and knocked hard. I heard someone curse before footsteps approached, and I took a step back, readying myself for what was to come. A middle-aged man opened the door, his shirt damp with a fresh coffee stain. His graying beard was overgrown and bushy. His eyes were wide with surprise as he took me in, but they were tired, with bags deeply ingrained in his skin. His remaining hair was white and frayed.

"Can I help you?" he asked. I didn't miss his annoyance.

I handed him the card I found in Abigail's coat. He scanned the card, grimaced, and told me to come inside. Without hesitation, I did. I didn't worry about my safety anymore. I just needed answers.

As I scanned the room, I was overwhelmed by the scent of stale cigarette smoke. The furniture was mismatched and clearly several years old, with worn cushions and mysterious stains. Knowing this was all Abigail could afford, I was embarrassed for her. He couldn't possibly be the best in the borough.

"What exactly can I help you with?" the man asked.

"I found that card on a friend of mine. Abigail Martin. I need to find her."

He arched a brow.

"What do you know about her?"

He grinned. "Sorry. Client privilege."

I groaned. I didn't have time for games. I needed answers, and I needed them now. I was on the brink of no return, and the slightest of breezes would push me over the edge. "Fine. I'd like to hire you to find my friend, Abigail Martin. Two down enough?"

"Two *thousand*?" he asked.

I nodded and pulled out a worn, thin checkbook from my jacket's inner pocket. Even though I never wrote checks, I always knew it'd come in handy to keep a few checks on me. "I can write you a check now or get you cash tomorrow. Either way, I expect work to begin immediately."

"Cash only."

"I have one thousand on me now," I said, withdrawing ten crisp one-hundred-dollar bills from my wallet's security pocket. I handed him the money. "I'll be back in a couple days for the information."

He nodded, and I turned to leave.

"You sure you want to find this girl?" he asked.

"Absolutely," I said without looking back.

CHAPTER EIGHTEEN

We walked in silence to the meeting house. It wasn't Sunday, when we normally held meetings, but Mother said there were important things to discuss with the community. I kicked the stones at my feet, annoyed I had to go with them. Normally, children didn't have to go. For every other meeting, I played outside after sermon. Sunday was the only day I didn't have chores, and this meeting was cutting into my play time.

I watched my friends playing kickball in the distance. Bobby waved me over, but I shook my head. I knew Mother wouldn't let me. No other kids were going to the meeting, but she said she didn't trust leaving me alone. I didn't understand what I'd done to make her not trust me anymore.

The meeting house looked just like all the other houses, except it was only one story and it was completely open on the main level. Instead of separate rooms, like a living room, kitchen, and dining area, it was a big, open space with rows of benches.

We walked inside, and I smiled at everyone I walked past. They were probably wondering what I was doing here. Maybe they could convince Mother to let me play outside. I considered asking someone to talk to her, but I decided against it. That would only upset Mother more, and she and Father were already angry all the time. Almost every day, I was told to go to my room. When they weren't looking, I'd sneak down a few stairs to listen to them, but they'd talk late into the night, and I'd get too sleepy to stay up with them until they went to bed.

The pastor stood at the front altar, busily trying to answer everyone's questions. So many were standing to shout, waving their arms at the pastor in anger. I wondered what we looked like to God in that moment. Would God be upset with us for yelling at His prophet?

My parents and I sat in the back row. I was thankful because our seats were closest to the open door. I hated the meeting house. After spending an hour listening to things I didn't understand, I was always drenched in sweat. Sometimes, the meetings ended too late in the day for a swim at the lake.

The windows were open, but the breeze never seemed to enter. I glanced over my shoulder, watching the long branches of a weeper blow in the distance. I whimpered, wishing I was outside.

"Why did you have us sign away our shares of the land and money?" someone yelled.

I slumped in my chair, listening as the pastor was compared to my parents. I crossed my arms over my chest, hoping I could just nap until the meeting was over.

"Maybe the Blakelys should take back control," another person said.

"Or maybe we should leave with them!"

I opened my eyes, looking around. Were we all leaving? Maybe we weren't leaving Living Light. Maybe we were relocating. I pulled on Mother's sleeve, trying to get her attention.

"Mother, are we moving Living Light? Are we going somewhere that's not so warm all the time?" I asked. I couldn't hide the giddiness in my voice. I'd prayed that was what we were doing. I loved it here, but it got too warm in the summer and too cold in the winter. If we all moved, we could start over somewhere else. We could bring Abi with us, too. I smiled at the idea.

"Hush, James," Mother said, wiggling her arm until I released her sleeve.

"But Momma," I said.

"James," Father said. It was enough to strike fear in my heart. Father was a gentle soul, but when he wanted to, he could scare the daylights out of me. I slouched in my chair, scanning the room. Maybe someone else would ask Mother if we were relocating.

My gaze landed on the pastor. I watched him as he wiped the sweat from his forehead with a small piece of cloth he kept in his pocket. His eyes were wide, fearful. He swallowed hard, and the lump in his throat bobbed. I'd never seen him look scared before. He looked mean sometimes and always calm but never afraid of what was to come. He was a prophet, after all. God guided him, telling him what the future held. Prophets were rarely terrified, I thought.

"No, no. No one has to leave. Everything will be fine. Just let me explain. Please."

He spent the next several hours trying to convince people not to leave. I didn't understand why he didn't want us to move where the weather was better, and every time I asked, Mother shushed me. Eventually, as the sun set, I closed my eyes and drifted to sleep, dreaming of nicer temperatures.

CHAPTER NINETEEN

NOW

The fan above me was spinning in circles, much like my life, each blade seemingly swiping toward me like a knife to the throat. The bed was hard, and it squeaked when I moved. The lumpy pillow had me lying at an awkward angle. I exhaled sharply as I tried to get comfortable. I hadn't thought much about the hotel I'd be staying at, so I took a room at the first one I found. I could practically feel the bed bugs crawling on me.

I closed my eyes, thinking about the mess I'd managed to get myself into. I couldn't understand why I didn't trust Jezebel with knowing my secrets. When she asked, I told her I was protecting her after everything she'd been through, but was that true? It was a pointless question because I already knew the answer. Deep down, I knew I'd once again lied to her.

I wasn't a dishonest man. In fact, I prided myself on my honesty. But I was ashamed of my past, of my behavior, and I hated the thought of disappointing her. Her judgment and disapproval of me seemed to fuel the fan above me. I closed my eyes, hoping the world around me would cease spinning out of control.

I woke with the sunlight hot on my face. Much to my surprise, I'd fallen asleep. I wiped the sleep from my eyes and sat up in bed, my feet planted firmly on the stained carpet of my hotel room. I grimaced at the thought of sleeping here, in this bed, another night and without Jezebel. I could handle the fact that this room had likely infected me with some incurable disease while I slept, but I couldn't handle a life without Jezebel.

I checked out of the hotel as quickly as I could. The clerk asked if I'd enjoyed my stay, and I fought back the urge to be honest. The thought of brutal honesty made my throat run dry. I didn't know this person, yet I was happy to *honestly* tell her how awful this hotel was, without regard to her feelings. Why couldn't I be as honest with Jezebel?

I stared at the door of our apartment. I wasn't sure how long it had taken to get here. I was a mindless drone, unthinking but never unmoving. I glanced down at the flowers in my hand. I barely remembered picking them up from a corner stand. Manhattan was a great city for buyers. It had everything from corporate stores to ma 'n' pa shops to street stands selling stolen or counterfeit goods.

Running a hand through my hair and then down my jacket, I tried to smooth my frayed and frazzled appearance. With only a few hours rest, no shower, and nothing but yesterday's alcohol in my system, I was sure I was one knock away from scaring the life from Jezebel.

She answered the door quickly, relief on her face. She didn't smile, but she didn't turn me away either.

"I was worried about you," she said as she pulled me into a hug.

I hugged her back, burying my face in her hair. She always smelled so good. Today, she smelled of vanilla and sunshine. She always smelled like sunshine. I had no other way to describe it, but her natural musk should be bottled and sold to the masses. It was a happy, relaxing, somewhat fruity smell, and I reveled in it.

"I'm sorry. I just needed...time."

She nodded against me, pulled me inside the apartment, and closed the door behind me.

"I'm so sorry, Jezebel," I said as I handed her the wildflowers I'd grabbed from the stand.

She smiled, smelled the flowers, and grabbed my hand. "They're beautiful," she said as we walked to the kitchen.

I watched her put them in a vase and rearrange them on the counter. The vase of roses I'd brought her only a few days ago was in the living room. I glanced at them. Their initial vibrancy had faded, and soon, they'd die.

I swallowed hard, fearing what I might say next. "Some things from my past have come back. I never meant to keep them from you. I just wanted to resolve them before involving you."

She nodded, her eyes still on the flowers I'd given her. She ran a thumb over a delicate petal, a frown sagging her beautiful features.

"I'm ashamed of myself for lying to you."

Her gaze met mine. "It's okay."

When it came to our pasts, Jezebel had always been forgiving. She had also buried her past, lying to everyone around her. I still remembered the haunting look on her face when she confessed her past sins to me.

When she was an undergrad in college, she had decided to attend a party to let off some steam. It wasn't in her nature, but final exams were stressful. She'd had too much to drink and had called her parents for a ride home. During the ride home, while nursing what she was sure would be a wicked hangover, she'd gotten into a fight with her parents. A drunk driver had crossed the median and crashed into their car. Her final words to her parents had been spoken in anger. She'd never forgiven herself for that moment.

She may not have driven the car that collided with and ultimately killed her parents, but she was the driver behind her hateful words and the cause for her parents to leave the house on that fateful night. I understood her pain, and deep down, I knew she understood why I had to deal with my past on my own terms.

"Come home," she whispered, threading her fingers with mine.

I looked down at our hands. Hers were small, soft, fragile in my own. That was our curse. She was delicate, while I was the beast.

"I can't. Not until I end this." It hurt to speak the truth, but separating from Jezebel while I tracked down Abigail was the right thing to do. It was the only way I could keep her safe, stop lying to her, and remove myself from the clutches of my past mistakes.

With tears threatening to spill, she looked at me, nodding. "I'll wait."

I kissed her with everything I had, hoping the kiss would speak for my silence.

CHAPTER TWENTY

Before I'd left Jezebel, I'd given her the address to the hotel I'd be staying at until this mess was cleaned up. It wasn't as disgusting or embarrassing as the place I'd stayed the night before. Rather than a one-star dive, this place was a four-star resort and much closer to our apartment. I could run to her place in fifteen minutes if she needed me.

A knock startled me as I unpacked the small bag I'd brought with me.

I peeked through the hole and exhaled sharply. Great. Just what I didn't need right now.

I was greeted with a nod after I opened the door. "Mr. Blakely."

"Detectives. How can I help you?"

"We stopped by your apartment, but Ms. Tate said you were staying here for a few days," Detective Montemurro said.

I nodded, not speaking, and I watched as Price peered past me, assessing my open bag and clothes that were strewn about on my bed.

"It's interesting that you'd stay in a hotel so close to your apartment," Detective Price said.

So, he speaks!

"Jezebel and I had a fight. We're taking some time apart."

They nodded in unison, as if a single being controlled them both. I saw a hint of a smile on Price's face and fought the urge to introduce his pearly whites to my fist.

"We're fine," I said, as if he even cared. I cleared my throat. "So, how can I help you, Detectives?"

"We'd like you to come with us," Price said.

I suppressed the gnawing sense of fear that threatened to overpower me. "Am I under arrest?"

"Of course not, but we need to get an official statement from you," Montemurro clarified.

"I thought this wasn't your case."

Price arched a brow in response. I was arousing suspicion. I knew that. But I didn't want to go to the police station and have an official record in place of my fucked-up past.

"It isn't, but we're assisting," Price said. "Since their time is better spent uncovering the truth at the scene—"

"And since you've been so cooperative up until this point—" Montemurro interrupted.

"We thought you'd be willing to help in any way you could. Is that a wrong assumption, Mr. Blakely?" Price finished.

He was trying to unnerve me, corner me into submission. Even though I wasn't a submissive man, I knew the police could make my life hell if I didn't cooperate, and since I had tried to illegally track Abigail with Reynolds's help, I wanted as few eyes on me and my whereabouts as possible.

"Of course not. I'm happy to help the investigation."

★ ★ ★

The problem with police station coffee, besides the fact that it tasted like shit, was that it was so dark it resembled tar. I imagined it coating my insides, taking years for the sludge-like substance to make its way through my system. If I was a conspiracy theorist, I'd think they'd made the coffee this way intentionally. The longer the caffeine took to work, the less alert I was during interrogation. The less alert I was, the more stupid shit came out of my mouth. It was simple mathematics, really.

"The DNA test confirmed your parents were among the dead."

I arched a brow. "Among the dead? You speak as if there are more than the two bodies."

They said nothing. This was an interrogation trick. Most people succumbed to silence, spilling their guts the moment things got awkward. But lately, my life was nothing but a sequence of awkward shit, so I was okay with the silence. I took a long, slow gulp of my tar.

"What can you tell us about the disappearance and death of your parents?" Montemurro asked.

I eyed the camera behind them. They'd asked if I was okay with them recording the interview. The detectives stuck miles away wanted a copy, since they couldn't be here themselves. Denying them would only raise suspicion. Maybe that was the lack of caffeine thinking...

I didn't answer their question, and I knew that looked bad, too. What could I say? Could I tell them the truth?

"Mr. Blakely?"

"I don't remember much," I lied.

"What do you remember?" Montemurro asked.

"My parents were good people."

"So how did two good people end up buried in the woods in upstate New York?" Price asked.

"Honestly, I have no idea."

That time, I told the truth. I didn't know how they ended up buried, because they weren't when I left. After I'd discovered their bodies, I'd run. I'd tried finding help, but I'd ended up getting lost in the woods. I wasn't sure how long I'd been out there, but eventually, someone had found me and brought me to the police station at a small town. I never spoke of what happened. I'd just...left them there. I swallowed down the bile that threatened to spill at the thought of what I'd done. What kind of person would leave their family and friends to rot in the wilderness?

"What do you know?" Price countered.

"My parents packed up their lives, bought a bunch of land, and moved to the middle of nowhere long before they had me. I grew up there, in this self-sufficient community. It was peaceful, and I loved it."

I took another gulp of my mud, and they waited for me to continue. I considered asking Price to fetch me a big-boy cup of coffee while the grownups talked this over, but I fought the urge.

"One day, a man came. He joined the community and took it to a...dark place." I played with the rim of my Styrofoam cup, digging the short tip of my nail into the side. "I don't remember much about him. He was a pastor, and that's what we called him. I never even learned his real name."

"Did this man hurt the people of the community?" Montemurro asked.

I glanced up, meeting the detective's eyes. How could I answer this question and not incriminate myself? If I was honest, then I was aware of a crime and did not report it. If I lied, well... Lying always caused more problems.

"In many ways, yes, he did."

"Tell us about him," Montemurro said.

I exhaled sharply, running a hand through my hair. "Honest. I don't know much about him. He was... He reminds me a lot of Charles Manson. In many ways, they're one and the same. Manson was able to convince his following to complete horrific acts in the name of their belief. He was...manipulative yet beautiful to his people. Parents would turn over their teen daughters to Manson, knowing full well what he planned to do to their bodies hours after they were introduced. The pastor was similar to Manson in a lot of ways. They were both monsters with the face of an angel. They both believed they were doing God's work."

"Do you know where this pastor is now?" Montemurro asked.

I shook my head. "For all I know, he's dead." I offered a silent prayer to God that that was the truth. It seemed God might be watching my back after all, so I hoped he heard this final prayer. After everything the pastor had done, he deserved to be rotting six feet under.

I spent the next several hours in that interrogation room, answering question after question, intentionally giving only enough information to satisfy their hunger without actually telling them the whole story. With each question asked, a small piece of my soul died. I was reliving the hell I'd been running from for so many years. I was one more question away from confessing just to make it end.

CHAPTER TWENTY-ONE

Mother told me this would be our last sermon. I'd cried myself to sleep the night before, praying to God this wasn't the truth. I didn't want to leave, and when I told Mother that, she simply smiled.

"I'm glad you loved living here, James."

She looked to my father, and something passed between them. I wasn't sure what it was, but it was a look I'd seen many times lately.

"I'm glad we made the right choice all those years ago. You were able to grow up happy, healthy."

"Why can't we stay?" I asked. If they loved it here so much, why were we leaving?

"It's not safe here anymore, James."

I groaned. I didn't understand this. For weeks, they'd whispered to each other about the safety of the community, but I hadn't noticed that anything had changed. Living Light was still the same happy place it had always been. Save for the pastor leading sermons, nothing had changed. I wasn't even marrying Abi anymore.

"Is this because I'm not doing God's work?" I asked. "I can marry Abi, Mother. I know I can do it."

She smiled softly, reached her hand out to me, and

caressed my cheek. Her eyes were bright with her tears. They pooled there, slowly streaking down her cheeks. I reached for one, stopping its escape with the tip of my finger.

"Why are you so sad, Mommy?" I asked.

She shook her head, quickly wiping away her tears. "I just love you so much, baby," she said.

"Do you know how proud we are of you, James?" Father asked.

I shook my head. "I thought you were upset with me." I swallowed hard. "I have a confession." I glanced away, unable to look them in their eyes. "I've broken a rule. I've disobeyed you."

"How so?" Father asked.

"When you tell me to go to my room at night, I only pretend to go. I sit at the top of the stairs and listen to you talk about Abi and me." I spoke so softly I could barely hear myself. I stared at the ground, ashamed of my sin. No wonder my parents didn't trust me to carry out God's plan; I couldn't even follow a simple rule to obey my elders.

"It's okay, James," Mother said.

I glanced up, feeling courageous. "Do you not trust me to marry Abi?"

She exhaled slowly. "James, God doesn't want you to marry Abi."

I gasped. "But he does!" The pastor said so. I knew this to be true.

Father walked over to me and rested a hand atop my shoulder. "One day, son, you'll understand what happened here. You'll see your mother and I only wanted the best for you. That's why we're leaving."

"It's my fault..." I whispered.

"It's not your fault, James. You did nothing wrong. Do you understand me?" Mother asked. She sounded angry, but I knew she wasn't.

I nodded, but it was a lie. I'd sinned again. Could I not stop? No wonder God didn't want me to marry Abi anymore. I wasn't worthy.

"Come. We'll be late for sermon," Mother said.

The door to our house slammed shut behind me. I'd slammed that door shut almost every time I left the house, but this time, it sounded louder. The crash echoed in my mind, making my head ache. We'd already packed what few belongings we had in sacks for our trip early in the morning. My sack was full of toys Bobby's mom had made for all the kids at Living Light. She loved to sew. She could make dolls and balls, and she made cars from wood. I didn't want to leave any behind, so I'd filled my sack with them, leaving my clothes in my drawers for Bobby to keep.

Slowly, I trudged toward the field where we held sermons when the weather was nice. Everyone was required to attend today. The pastor said he had a special ceremony to honor and say goodbye to those who were leaving with us. I thought it was nice, but I was really sad to leave Abi behind. I knew I'd never see her again. I wondered if she'd miss me, too.

When we arrived, we sat on the ground at the back of the group. Normally, we sat in the front row, but I didn't complain. From back here, I could watch others without anyone noticing.

"Welcome, and thank you for joining me today. It is my greatest privilege to honor the Blakely family, as well as those who've helped to bring together this community of truly remarkable individuals and families."

The pastor smiled brightly. I watched as he moved. He

seemed...different. He was oddly happy, but Abi, beside him, cowered in her seat. She didn't meet my eyes—or anyone else's for that matter. I waved at her, trying to get her attention, but she never looked my way.

"We are an eclectic group, our love of God bringing us together. I know not all Christian traditions practice the ceremony of communion, but I thought this would be a wonderful way to honor those we're losing tomorrow morning."

Mother glanced at Father, who kept his eyes on the pastor. I wasn't sure what "communion" was, but if it was a way to honor God and the people at Living Light, I would do it. I would do anything to prove to God that He could trust me again and use me as his tool. I knew He didn't want me to marry Abi anymore, because Mother said so, but it saddened me that He'd lost faith in me. I would prove I was devoted to anything He wanted me to do.

"Please, stand and join me."

One by one, members of the community stood in line, taking a small piece of bread from the pastor and drinking a small sip of wine from a chalice Abi held. When done, each returned to their seat on the grass.

The sun was hot on my skin, and I shielded it from my eyes when I looked out at the open field in the distance. I was sad to leave here but excited to start somewhere anew. My parents had built a beautiful community here, so I was sure they could do it again. I tried to stay positive, hoping that would make me miss those who stayed behind less.

When it was our turn, the pastor handed me a small piece of bread. I glanced at Mother and smiled, but she was too busy looking at the others to notice me.

In a moment too quick for my young eyes, Mother

smacked the piece of bread from my hands as I brought it to my lips. I noticed it smelled funny just before it flew through the air and fell to the ground several feet away from me. My skin stung where her hand had struck mine.

I looked up in time to see the pastor strike Mother. She cried out, falling to the ground. I screamed, dropping to my knees beside her. I wanted to pull her close to me, shield her from this demon and beg it to hurt me instead. I crouched in front of her, covering her with my arms. Her eyes watered where the pastor's fist had landed. Her skin turned red as she covered it with her hand.

"Run, James. Hide. And do not eat or drink anything from anyone!" Mother said, her breath hot on my skin.

She tried to yell, but her voice shook. I couldn't understand her words. Why did she want me to run and hide? I would protect her.

I scanned the area for Father, finding him several feet away, rolling around on the ground with the pastor. They fought, each slamming their fists against the other.

"Stop!" I yelled. "Don't hurt him!"

I ran to him, trying to pull the pastor away. He'd had Father pinned to the ground, his hands smacking Father's face over and over again. I dug my nails into the flesh of his cheeks, yanking my hands back until I reached his hair. I pulled it as hard as I could, and he cried out.

"No!" Mother yelled when the pastor's elbow struck me.

I fell backward, my chest heaving at the contact. In a quick, sharp jab, the pastor sent all the air from my lungs. I gasped for breath and dug my fingers into my skin as if I could rip open my chest for the air to reach my lungs more easily.

"Run, James!" Mother yelled as she stood.

I climbed to my feet, running until I tripped. I rose again, dusting the dirt from my hands. All around me, people were slumped over. No one spoke. No one moved. No one looked at me. I didn't understand what had happened. Why was no one helping us?

I ran to Bobby, grabbing on to his arm and telling him to run with me. I yanked on him, and he fell forward. He slouched against his mom's lap. His eyes were open but lifeless. He didn't blink. He didn't move.

"Bobby!" I screamed, trying to wake him.

I knew he was dead. I knew they were all dead, but a small, hopeful part of me prayed they were just playing a cruel game.

Scared, I dropped his arm and ran for the woods. I heard Mother call for me in the distance, but I didn't turn back. I ran until my legs ached and my chest heaved. I ran until I couldn't breathe, couldn't think, couldn't hear the screams of my parents any longer.

CHAPTER TWENTY-TWO

Now

The sunshine on my face was a lie. It was telling me to be happy, to enjoy my time on earth while I still had a life to live. It didn't know the demons within me were awakening, ready to play. Or maybe it did, but it didn't care. This was my penance—to be forever at the mercy of my sins.

My feet slammed against the pavement as I left the police station. They let me go but made it clear I wasn't to leave town. I wasn't under arrest, but I was a suspect. Maybe if I'd told them everything, instead of bits of pieces of the truth, they wouldn't think that. Or maybe they'd look at me the way I feared Jezebel would look at me when she learned the truth, when she learned I'd been lying about so much for so long. Like with the police, I'd only shared bits and pieces of my past with her. Even so, it was more than I'd ever told anyone before.

I found my way into a corner dive bar and took a seat on an open stool.

"Whiskey. Straight," I said to the bartender who was drying a glass he'd just washed. He placed it in front of me and poured a splash of amber liquor into it.

"Double," I added, and he poured more.

I drank it quickly, slamming the glass onto the counter when I was finished.

"Another," I said, my voice cracking as the smooth liquid coated my throat. It burned in all the right ways. He poured me another double, and I downed it. Starting to feel at ease, I simply nodded at the man. He poured a final glass before returning the whiskey to the glass shelf behind him.

"Long day?" he asked before returning to cleaning glasses.

"I don't wanna talk about it," I slurred. I wasn't drunk— yet—but I was feeling the effects of top-shelf alcohol. Slowly, it was warming my insides, washing away the shitty coffee and morning accusations. The last thing I wanted to do was spill my secrets to a fucking bartender. I sipped my drink, exhaling sharply as it hit the spot. "Good whiskey."

The bartender nodded. I threw down a couple fifties to ease his nerves. I grabbed my cup and turned toward the room. There was never an empty bar in Manhattan. It didn't matter if it was two in the morning, noon, or five at night, someone always needed a pick-me-up at the bar. As I watched a few men play a game of pool, generously swigging beer from their bottles, I thought about what might have brought them here. Surely they hadn't been taken in by the police and forced to relive their worst memories. Or hell, maybe they had been. After all, Price was a dick.

I scanned the room. The walls of the bar were littered with neon signs and old album covers. There were a few corner tables, but other than that, the only seating was at the bar; the floor space was filled with rows of pool tables. Apparently, this was a bar for pool leagues.

A woman's laugh caught my attention. It was deep and throaty, and it unnerved me. She was at a corner table, sitting on a man's lap. She looked at least a decade younger than him, but that was likely a bad judgment call. Women seemed to age better than men, so maybe he was the younger of the two.

She swiveled her hips, rubbing her ass against his crotch. I felt my own cock stir in response. I took another drink, unable to look away. He reached forward and caressed her breast with one hand. The other still rested at her waist, but I was sure it would soon move, only this time, lower.

Like clockwork, he reached down, cupping her pussy under her skirt. Maybe it was all the time I'd spent at the police station today that was making me such a damn good detective. She gasped as his arm flexed, and I imagined him sliding his finger deep inside her. She bit her lower lip. Her teeth dragged against the skin there. I inhaled sharply, my breath slamming into me like a taxi cab during rush hour. It was brief, painful, and left me feeling like a fucked-up pervert.

I spun in my chair, setting my empty glass on the countertop.

"Another?" the bartender asked.

I didn't answer. Instead, I thought about Jezebel. I desperately wanted to be near her. I needed to hear her voice, feel her touch. I wanted to kiss her, touch her, be with her.

But she didn't deserve this, or me, or my fucked-up past. She was finally getting her life together after her attack, with her writing, film deals, and high-class parties. She was too good for me. Eventually, she'd see that too.

My phone vibrated in my pocket. Jezebel's name lit up my screen, and in a moment so brief I had to question if it really happened, I thought about ignoring her call, leaving, and never returning. She'd be better off without me. But I was a coward. I'd always been a weak man—strong physically but weak in all that truly mattered.

"Jez?" I said softly.

"Hello, Jamesy," a voice said. It was soft yet powerful, and it shook me to my core. A name I hadn't heard in years had come back to poison me with the sins of my past.

"Abigail?" I whispered. I spoke so softly I wasn't sure I actually said anything at all.

"I'm glad we could finally get back in touch. I heard you've been looking for me."

"Where's Jezebel?" I asked with newfound confidence.

She laughed, a slow, deep, malevolent sound that surely matched the smile she'd offered me days ago. "She's with me, of course."

I swallowed hard and chose my next words carefully. "Have you hurt her?"

She breathed sharply into the phone. "Not yet, but I will. Oh, you know I will. Don't you, Jamesy?"

"Yes," I said carefully, because she was right. I knew she would. With her father's blood coursing through her veins, I knew she was capable of the most heinous acts.

"We're going to play a game, Jamesy. I remember how much you used to love games." I could hear her smile through the phone. It coated her words in wicked cheerfulness. It was a sobering slap in the face.

"Don't hurt her," I said slowly.

"Then I guess you'd better hurry over. You have ten minutes, Jamesy."

"And if I can't make it in ten minutes?"

"I think you know what will happen if you're late."

My phone went silent, the screen dark after the call ended. I shoved it into my pocket and ran as though my life depended on it. Because it did. Jezebel *was* my life, and I would do whatever needed to be done to keep her safe.

CHAPTER TWENTY-THREE

Now

I'd rarely experienced true panic. Even in one of the most dangerous careers, I seldom let my emotions overcome my thinking. But now, as the rain began to fall, I couldn't deny I was scared shitless. The rain quickened, splattering against my hot skin. My clothes were sopping, my hair clinging to my forehead. Streams of salty sweat stung my eyes as I tried to blink away the rain pouring down. My body ached. I was exhausted, starving, dehydrated, a little buzzed, and a lot annoyed. Abigail couldn't have chosen a more perfect time to make her move.

I was off my game, and a simple mistake could cost Jezebel her life. I hadn't forgiven myself for the torture she endured at Miller's hands. I'd lowered my guard, and she'd been taken. I wouldn't let that happen again. I wasn't sure what Abigail had planned, but I wasn't naïve to her malevolent nature.

I needed to quicken my pace. I put everything I had into running. My legs felt like they would give way to fatigue at any moment, but I prayed they wouldn't.

I pushed through a crowd of people. A woman spun on her heels, grabbing on to me and bringing us both to the ground in a thump. She cried out, pushing me off her and smacking me with the handle of her umbrella as if I were attacking her.

I breathed an apology before taking off again, leaving her on the ground. I couldn't worry about her. I had to get to Jezebel.

When I reached our building, I knew it had to have been more than ten minutes. Two at a time, I took the stairs up the three flights. I crashed through the unlocked door. My chest was heaving. Sweat and rainwater dripped steadily down my skin. My clothes were heavy. Too heavy. I needed to be light, limber, ready to pounce, not weighed down by a soaked suit. My legs ached, and my heart dropped at the sight of our living room.

The furniture had been tossed around. Jezebel's artwork was on the floor, large slashes in each frame. Glassware from the kitchen lay in smashed piles around the room, shards of glass stuck in the fabric of the couch. The vases of flowers I'd given Jezebel seemed to have been thrown across the room and into the wall. Thick lines of dripping water streaked the paint. Jezebel's laptop sat atop a corner table. It was open, the screen shattered.

In the center of the room, where I'd normally find the backs of two decorative chairs, was Jezebel. She was sitting on a stool, her hands behind her back, one of my ties covering her mouth. Black tears streamed from her eyes, leaving dark gray streaks in their wake. I took a step toward her and saw movement out of the corner of my eye.

Before I could react, Abigail had her arms around me, pulling me close to her. I went rigid. I couldn't move, couldn't think.

"I've waited *so* long for this moment, Jamesy."

I nodded, my chin rubbing against the top of her head. My eyes were on Jezebel. I tried to convey that she was going to be fine, that I would keep her safe. Jezebel was a fighter, and

I knew she would lash out at Abigail the moment she could. Without speaking, I tried to tell her to remain calm, to do nothing. I mouthed that I loved her. She sniffled and nodded.

"I've been telling Jezebel all about our wedding. How we've been planning it for such a long time."

I frowned. "Our wedding?"

"It's okay, Jamesy. Jezebel knows about us now, about how we're destined to be together. I've waited for you, to marry you, like God wanted."

I looked into her eyes as she pulled back from me. She was about an arm's length away, but everything had changed. She wasn't a psychotic stalker intent on revenge. She was a mentally ill girl, damaged by the actions of her father. She was...like me. Marred by her father's actions.

"Abigail, you and I are not getting married." I spoke slowly, hoping she could process each and every word.

She took several steps back, furrowing her brow. She looked at me as if she truly couldn't comprehend my words. All these years I'd feared her, she was nothing but a lost girl in search of her truth.

"Marriage is about love, and I love Jezebel."

I watched as Abigail's features changed from confusion to pain to anger. She'd taken so many steps backward that she now stood just behind Jezebel.

"You love *her*? Are you going to marry her, Jamesy?" Her voice cracked, and it made my chest hurt.

"Abigail..." I said softly.

"No! Answer my question!" she yelled.

In a movement too quick for my sleepy eyes, Abigail stepped closer to Jezebel, withdrew a knife, and pushed it against Jezebel's neck. Jezebel squealed as the blade moved against her skin, a single crimson drop sliding down her neck.

"Stop!" I yelled, taking a step forward.

"If you come any closer, I *will* kill her."

I halted, waiting for her next order. I was at the mercy of her blade.

"Answer me. Are you marrying *her*?"

"No..." I spoke slowly, carefully, hoping I didn't bring Abigail to the edge.

Jezebel sniffled, but I couldn't bring myself to look her in the eyes. I was watching Abigail, focusing on her every move. I watched her muscles tighten in response to my answer. Her eyes narrowed, her breathing hitched. I watched every move, searching for any sign she might yank the blade across Jezebel's soft, smooth skin. In all my years of military training, I'd become good at anticipating an opponent's next move. I hoped this skill wouldn't fail me today.

"You and I, we're leaving together," she said, her voice dangerously low. Little did she know, that was exactly what I wanted.

I nodded. "Yes, come with me, Abi." I used the name I used to call her, hoping it would spark something within her. She smiled, and the pressure of the blade on Jezebel's neck released ever so slightly.

"We'll get married?" she asked.

I pressed my lips together and nodded. I hated lying to her. Even she deserved better. "Let's go now." I offered her my hand. "We can go straight to the courthouse. Come with me."

She snorted. "Oh, Jamesy. I knew you were in love with me." She bit her lower lip, and I felt queasy. "But we can't get married without Daddy."

I inhaled sharply, my breath seething through my teeth. My sputtering heart seemed to slow in that moment. "Daddy?

He's...alive?"

Abigail nodded enthusiastically, like a bobblehead toy on the dash of a Manhattan taxi. "He'll be so excited when we tell him we're finally getting married."

"I think your daddy should marry us," I said. My hands were in fists at my sides. My shock dissipated, and all I could feel in that moment was pure rage.

Abigail gasped. "Yes! That would be perfect."

"I think you should take me to Daddy, Abi."

She nodded again, smiling.

"Let's go now. Daddy's waited so long. I think he'll be happy to see us together."

"Okay," she squeaked. She stepped away from Jezebel, knife in hand, and walked toward me. "Let's go, Jamesy." She grabbed my hand, linking her fingers between my own. Unlike Jezebel's soft, smooth hands, Abigail's were rough, dry, cracked. It felt unnatural to have them there, and I shook the desire to rip my hand free from her clutches.

As I turned to leave with her, I offered Jezebel one final, parting goodbye. We didn't speak, but the pain in her eyes matched the pain in my heart. In our silence, I tried to convey that I loved her, that she would be okay, and I had to go now. I had to finish this. She nodded, tears streaming down her cheeks.

The door slammed shut behind me, and hand in hand with Abigail, I went to the man who'd stolen everything from me.

CHAPTER TWENTY-FOUR

By the time I found the courage to walk back home, the sun was low in the sky. I shivered, the night air much cooler than the day's heat.

I saw them in the distance. No one had moved. Their bodies were limp, right where they had been. I walked slowly, scanning my surroundings with each step I took, but I knew I was alone. I whimpered, tears streaming down my cheeks, as I stepped over the bodies. Everyone was here, but no one was left.

Some of my friends' eyes were still open. They had been taken so quickly they didn't have time to blink. Their usually bright eyes were turning a cloudy white, a color so haunting I shut my eyes closed to shake it. I knew this sight would stay with me until the day I died.

"Mommy?" I said, my voice cracking. "Daddy?"

No one responded. I kept walking until I reached the front of the group, where Father and the pastor had had their scuffle. Tears stung as I fell to their sides, knees buckling under my weight.

Mother died with her arm reaching for Father, whose neck was bruised with two small blue circles. His face was puffy, and he looked nothing like the man I'd known all my life.

I reached for Mother. Her skin was cold. I nudged her.

"Mommy?"

I nudged her again. Her body was stiff, her eyes closed, her chest unmoving.

"Please wake up," I whispered. Snot bubbled from my nose, and I wiped it with the back of my hand, hiccupping as I sucked in breath through my mouth.

I heard a noise in the distance. It sounded like a branch snapping. I shot to my feet and squinted, trying to see past the tree line. With the setting sun, I saw nothing. I turned on my heel and ran. I dashed beyond the safety of the brush and ran until the night made running too hard. I walked then, never unmoving. I didn't know where I was going, but I had to get away.

I shivered under the moon's glow and pulled my arms to my chest, trying to stay warm. Another snap of a branch had me crying out. I slammed into a tree and then climbed it until I couldn't get any higher. I sat, straddling the branch and leaning against the thick trunk. I was high up, and I felt safe.

Someone was coming. I jerked my head at every noise, and my heart raced. I didn't think I'd ever stop crying, but soon, my eyes tired and I drifted to sleep.

I woke and jolted upright while reaching out frantically. I'd shifted in my sleep, but I hadn't fallen from my makeshift bed. My eyes were tired, my stomach was rumbling from hunger, and my back ached from the long night.

I climbed down, jumping to the ground when I was low enough. I slammed onto my butt and cried out when I fell. My legs hurt so bad I was sure I couldn't walk another step, but I did. I never looked back but was always watching my surroundings. I couldn't shake the feeling that I wasn't alone, that someone was watching me.

When I reached a stream, I fell to my knees and drank handful after handful of water. I hadn't realized I was so thirsty, but it felt like I hadn't drunk water in days. When I'd had my fill and glanced around, my heart nearly fell from my chest when our gazes met.

"Are you okay?" the man asked.

I didn't know who he was, so I jumped to my feet and ran. I glanced back, watching him as I retreated. I smacked into something and fell to the ground. Dazed, I looked up. The sun was bright above me, and I raised my arm to shield my eyes. Another man towered before me. He leaned in, blocking the sun.

"Hey, it's okay. We won't hurt you," he said. His voice was soft, kind.

I scooted on my butt, trying to escape him, but it was no use. I was trapped between the two.

"Are you alone?" one asked.

I didn't answer as I stood. I didn't know what to do. Did I run? Did I hide? Did I fight?

"Are you hungry? We have some food."

I remembered what Mother told me. I wasn't to eat anything anyone gave me, but I was so hungry. My stomach hurt so bad I thought I would die. I nodded, ashamed of my weakness.

"Okay, I'm going to reach inside my bag. I have some energy bars. You can have some. Sound good, kid?"

I nodded again, watching as he slowly reached into his bag and tossed me a few small packages of food. They scattered on the ground at my feet. I looked at them, confused. What were these? I picked up one and stared at it. I'd never seen food in a casing like this.

"Just rip it open."

I tried to tear at its covering, but it wouldn't budge.

"Would you like me to help you?"

I swallowed and nodded. Slowly, he closed the distance between us. When he reached me, I offered him the food. He ripped it open with ease and handed it back to me. I brought it to my nose, closed my eyes, and inhaled deeply. It smelled weird, but I was starving. I devoured it quickly, my stomach turning at its dry taste. The man opened the others for me, and I swallowed them down just as quickly.

"Where are your parents?"

I chewed the final bites of the bar, not answering his question. I didn't want to think about them. I didn't want to talk about it.

"I think we should call the cops, man."

"We don't get service out here, remember?"

I tossed the wrappers on the ground, and the man leaned over to pick them up. He shoved them into his pockets and smiled at me.

"We don't want to litter, little man." His floppy black hair fell into his eyes, and he pushed it to the side with the flick of his head. His eyes were so dark they looked almost black, but when the sun hit them, I could tell they were a really dark brown. It was unnerving. He looked almost demonic. Briefly, I wondered if I should trust him or if he was another test from God.

"Are you alone?" he asked.

I nodded.

"Would you like to stay with us?"

I swallowed and nodded. I didn't want to be alone. I hadn't

seen the pastor or Abi with my parents in the field, and I was sure they were out here, looking for me. If they found me and I wasn't alone, maybe they wouldn't hurt me. My chest ached when I thought about my parents. I felt guilty for leaving them, but I was scared to go back. What if the pastor waited for me there?

"I think we should take him to the police. I saw a sign for a town when we turned down that little side road. I don't think it was too far. Maybe someone there knows him," the other man said.

I didn't look at him. I didn't know how to tell him that no one knew me. I was alone. Forever.

CHAPTER TWENTY-FIVE

Now

Abigail took me to a flashy, high-rise apartment building in the middle of one of Manhattan's most expensive neighborhoods. The gray building was nearly wall-to-wall windows. As we stood in front of the doors, I saw nothing but my own reflection in them. My clothes were still damp, my hair frizzing as it dried. Save for my suit, I looked like a homeless person. Abigail looked well put together, but I wondered if they'd let both of us in the building. I was sure there was a dress code just to stand in the lobby, and I was sure it didn't include yesterday's clothes cleaned by today's rain shower.

"Your father lives here?" I asked, scanning the expanse of the high-rise.

In her window's reflection, I watched her nod in response.

Anger boiled in the pit of my gut. This apartment would cost him millions of dollars. Could he have afforded this if not for the families he murdered and robbed? Had our land and our possessions afforded him this lavish lifestyle? Had my parents died for this?

"Come on, Jamesy," Abigail said, pulling me toward the door.

We entered the lobby. Abigail's shoes smacked against the marble floors until we reached the elevators. Each clunk of her sandal drew more unnecessary attention to us, to me. I shouldn't be here—not with only my intentions fueling me.

"Ms. Martin." Abigail was greeted by the attendant, who pressed the button for the penthouse suite.

I suppressed the urge to punch the wall. As the doors closed, I was offered my reflection once again. Everything in this building was shiny, polished, expensive. I gritted my teeth, jaw clenched, as I thought about meeting her father again.

In all the years I'd lived with the memories of my past, I never thought about seeing him again. I was sure he wasn't even alive. I hadn't heard anything about him or the community. I'd researched it once. The land had slowly been sold to multiple buyers. Most of the land was left intact. Each sale was done for under-assessed value and in cash, so I couldn't trace anything without raising suspicion. But that was years ago. How had we been living in the same city all this time? Did he know I was here, too?

The elevators pinged, and we stepped into the foyer of the penthouse apartment.

"Daddy?" Abigail called. Her hand was slick in my own, and I wondered if it was from my sweat or hers. Was she just as nervous as I was?

A muffled greeting came from a distance.

"He's in the living room," Abigail said, dragging me through a hallway.

As we walked from room to room, one thing was clear. This man was not struggling. The expensive look of the building didn't end at the lobby. His floors were of the same marble, with swirling whites and grays. His walls were a ridiculous shade of white that was probably marketed with an equally absurd name, like Angel Kiss. Walls that weren't lined with floor-to-ceiling breathtaking views of Manhattan were cluttered with paintings. I didn't know much about art, but I did know it was an expensive hobby for collectors.

We walked into the living room, and I saw him. He stood in the far corner, staring out through his wall of windows. He was a king in his castle as he looked out at his domain. And I was here as the Trojan horse.

He sipped a cocktail. His back was to us, but I still assessed him. He was dressed casually and was thinner than I remembered. Even across the room, I could see he was shorter than me. Had he always looked this weak? Had his power truly been in only his words?

"Daddy, I have a surprise for you," Abigail said cheerfully.

He turned, and our gazes locked. He had just taken a sip of his drink, and he hacked. I prayed he'd choke on it. I smiled as he fought to catch his breath, his eyes watering as the alcohol burned his lungs. I imagined his pain. Alcohol burning your lungs couldn't be a pleasant feeling.

"Abigail," he said. His voice was weak as he tried to catch his breath. I was sure the alcohol still burned, and I took great pleasure in that. I never knew I could be such a sadist.

"Are you okay, Daddy?"

She dropped my hand and rushed to his side. Finally, I was free of her. I rubbed the sweat from my hands onto my pants. My arms were weak. I felt like I'd been squeezing my hands in fists since I'd arrived at Jezebel's and my apartment.

She leaned against him, grabbing on to his arm to support him, but he pushed her away.

"You brought *him* here? Are you fucking stupid?" he screamed.

She gasped, her eyes wide as she stumbled backward. I

wondered if that was the first time he'd ever spoken to her in anger. I doubted that. He seemed like a weak man who used his words to belittle her.

"Why would you bring him here?"

"I found him, Daddy. I found him so we could finish God's work. We have to get married. We wanted you to marry us, Daddy." She smiled widely, her eyes brightening at the idea of marrying me.

The pastor took a step back, shock plastered on his face. He stared into Abigail's eyes before his gaze dropped to give her a once-over. In that moment, it was like he was seeing her—*really* seeing her—for the first time. She was so honest, so completely sure that marrying me was what she wanted. She had no idea the decision to marry me was never truly her own. She was utterly faithful to the dishonest and manipulative man before her, and she had no idea that he never truly cared for her, her future, or to whom he gave her hand in marriage. She'd been a tool for him, and now he could finally see how his past shaped her future.

"Abigail..." His voice was low, soft, nearly inaudible.

She frowned. "Are you unhappy with me, Daddy? I thought this was what you wanted."

He shook his head. "I don't want you to marry him. Not anymore. You deserve better. Don't you see that?"

"But I love him, Daddy. You told me to love him, and I did. I've loved him for all these years."

I swallowed, my heart aching for her. I'd spent my life cursing her name. Knowing she was out there, writing a blog about her father's role in the massacre of my family and friends, caused me to carry such hate, such uncontrollable anger for her. But she was not what I was expecting.

"You don't love him. Do you understand me?"

She opened her mouth to speak but said nothing as she looked at both of us. Her gaze darted back and forth as she tried to understand what was happening. In that moment, I wondered how many other families and communities the pastor had tried to rob. How many other times had he used his impressionable daughter as a pawn in his game? How could he be so shocked that her psyche had broken under the weight he bestowed upon it?

"I don't love him?" she asked.

"No," the pastor said.

In a fit of rage, she pulled a small handgun from the waist of her jeans. It had been hidden by the sweater she wore that covered the small of her back. I gasped at the sight of her pulling the gun and pointing it at her father, who looked equally as shocked.

"You lie!" she yelled.

He raised his hands in the air, likely by instinct, and spoke calmly. "I'm sorry, Abigail. I didn't mean to scare you. It was a test, of course. A test from God."

"A test?" she asked quietly. "From God?"

He nodded. "God needed to know you were devoted to his cause." The pastor took a step toward her. "And you are. I can see that now. I'm sorry." He cleared his throat. "I'm sorry I doubted you."

She smiled, her hand wavering.

"You and James can be together. Forever. But..."

"But what?" she asked.

"You'll have to wait. God wants James to be with him now."

I balled my fists at my sides as I listened to his words. Was he seriously going to try to manipulate her into shooting me?

"It's time James joined the community, in heaven, with God."

Abigail smiled, nodding her understanding.

"Don't listen to him, Abi," I said as I stepped forward. "He's lying to you. He's always lied to you."

"The Devil shows himself in many ways," the pastor said, looking at me. "He forces you to question your faith in God, in God's plan." He took another step forward, and I matched his move. We were only a few feet apart now.

"I will not be swayed by the Devil! I will do as God asks of me. James and I will both be together forever," Abigail screamed.

The reality of her words shook me to my very core.

"No!" I said, lunging toward her. I reached her just as a gunshot echoed through the apartment. In a loud clunk, the weapon fell to the ground beside her. I dove forward, catching her before she hit the ground. She sank into my arms, the light in her eyes waning as she gasped for breath.

"Abigail!" the pastor yelled.

I glanced at the gun, but with Abigail in my arms, I wasn't sure I could reach it before the pastor got to it first.

"You!" His voice was dark, deep, a hateful accusation coating the word.

He lunged for the gun, and I dropped Abigail, praying I could reach it first.

In the silence of the apartment, a second gunshot pierced the room, cutting thickly, deeply, until nothing could be heard, save for the abating beats of a stilling heart.

CHAPTER TWENTY-SIX

Now

He was curled into a ball on the floor, crying while nursing his leg, and I was shaking, fighting every urge not to pull the trigger again. In our scuffle for the gun, I'd shot him in his leg. Sadly, I'd missed his femoral artery. I couldn't keep my arm straight as I kept the gun pointed at him. It would be so easy, *so easy*, to end his trail of destruction right now. After all, he didn't deserve to live.

I pressed the trigger ever so slightly, feeling it give way beneath my finger. An ounce more of pressure would release the bullet that was itching to leave the chamber. I'd always been taught that if I pointed a gun at something, I'd better be ready to destroy everything in its path. And I was. I was more than ready to avenge the death of every single person this pathetic excuse of a pastor had murdered.

My gaze flickered to Abigail. She was lifeless on the ground. Her eyes were open, facing the ceiling, though I knew she no longer saw it. After years of living with a sociopath, she'd suffered the mental consequences. The regret and despair I felt for her clung to me, and I feared I'd never shake it.

"You didn't deserve her," I said as I looked at him.

My phone buzzed in my pocket, a jolting sensation that brought me back to this moment. I pulled it free, keeping the gun pointed at the man I was sure was the Devil himself. Jezebel's face lit up my screen.

"Jezebel," I whispered.

"James? James! Oh my God. Where are you? Are you okay?" She sounded frantic, but I couldn't worry about that right now. Still, I was thankful she had been freed. When I left her, I assumed Abigail's restraints weren't enough to truly hold Jezebel captive. She'd nearly escaped Miller, who'd put greater effort into containing her.

"I can't stop myself," I whispered.

"James? Tell me where you are. Please."

"With *him*." My voice was sinister, and it surprised me. I'd never heard such hate escape my lips.

"Where? Where is he?"

"I can't... I have to do this. You understand that I have to do this?" I was desperate for her approval because I wasn't sure I could stop even if she withheld it.

She sobbed into the phone. "Please, James. Please come home to me."

"He killed her. He killed them all."

"Who? Abigail? He killed her?"

I nodded.

"James? Are you there?"

I inhaled sharply. "He killed her. His own daughter. He kills everyone he meets. I have to stop him."

I needed to do this. For Abi, the girl who spent her life loving him, believing in him, worshiping him. For the many faceless victims I didn't know but was sure existed.

I needed to do this for my parents.

My arm ached. Every fiber of my being told me to lower the weapon, to call the police, to turn him in, and to go home to Jezebel. But even though the rational part of my brain screamed at me, I didn't want to listen to it.

I'd never thought about what I'd say—or do—to the man who destroyed my life, because I never thought I'd be granted the opportunity to face him again. But here, now, as he whimpered on the ground like the bitch he was, I was overwhelmed with a sense of power. And he needed to be stopped.

"James! Listen to me."

I blinked. Once. Twice. My breath hitched. I'd killed many people before. In the military, my team was known for covert operations. We were closers. We were sent to do what needed to be done for the sake of freedom, safety, and security. I'd pulled the trigger on countless terrorists to save my brethren— never giving the decision to end a life a second thought. I'd never lost a night's rest over my actions either because I truly believed I was doing the right thing. Sometimes, to save a life, you must take one. Sometimes, the balance must be restored.

I could do it again. The man cowering before me was no different than the men I'd killed as a marine. Hell, I was sure I'd killed better men than him.

"He killed them, Jez. I watched him kill my family. He did it with a smile on his face and a song in his heart." Tears threatened to spill as I remembered that day. He was an animal on a mission to live a luxury life by stealing from others. "He needs to be put down."

"James, I know how much this hurts."

She did. Her parents had been killed by a drunk driver who'd fathered a son so deranged he'd kidnapped and tortured Jezebel years later. What kind of man produced such an offspring? Jezebel had confronted her demons the moment she discovered Miller was that man's son.

"You did it," I whispered.

"I had no choice. You do. You know you don't have to do this, James."

I swallowed hard as I listened to her. She was trying desperately to save my soul, but I was already at the edge, ready to fall into the abyss. And I wanted nothing more than to take this monster with me straight to hell.

"If you do this, you are no better than him. You've stopped him, James. Killing him now is no better than what he did to your family, to all those innocent people, all those years ago."

That was a knife to the gut, a crash back to reality.

"Come home to me, baby."

I nodded and hung up. She was right. I wasn't God. Taking God's work into my own hands would make me no better than the monster before me. I wouldn't offer him the pleasure of becoming his protégé.

"That was Jezebel," I said as I dialed a three-digit number. "She's...incredible. The strongest person I know." I sniffled and exhaled slowly as I pressed to call the number. "She saved my life just now. In jail, you're given one phone call. You should call and thank her." I lowered the gun. "Because she saved yours, too."

The dispatcher greeted me, and I told her our location. In less than fifteen minutes, the apartment was swarming with police and emergency medical technicians. I offered my statement, this time withholding nothing, as the two detectives who'd been interviewing me listened, scribbling down every word. I watched as Abigail's body was carted away and the pastor's leg was wrapped before he was handcuffed and loaded onto a wheeled stretcher. An officer placed the gun I'd used into a clear evidence bag, and I glanced down, staring at my hands.

"Mr. Blakely?"

I glanced up.

"You did the right thing," Detective Montemurro said.

I exhaled slowly, nodding. "I know. Thanks, Detective."

"You need to get checked out by an EMT, and then you can head home. We'll follow up with you tomorrow," Price said.

I stood, my body stiff, and left the apartment with the detectives. The rain had stopped, and the sun was shining. The concrete, dark gray from the rain, looked clean, new, as if the grime of the New York City streets had been washed away.

I walked over to an available emergency technician and mindlessly followed each of his instructions. In the end, I was cleared to go home.

My phone buzzed, and I quickly yanked it from my pocket, hoping to see Jezebel's name light up my screen. Instead, I saw an unfamiliar number.

"Hello?" My voice was gruff, strained, and only then did I realize how exhausted I was.

"Mr. Blakely? It's Mr. Smith."

I didn't respond.

"Your PI."

"Yes, I know who you are."

"Well, I got some info back that you might be interested in. Seems Ms. Martin has spent quite a few years in a psych ward. Her father, Patrick Martin, funded her stays. They have quite a few overseas accounts with several million dollars in them."

"Mr. Smith, thanks for your help, but you can stop investigating. It's over."

It was *finally* over.

CHAPTER TWENTY-SEVEN

The door was flung open, and she pulled me into a tight hug. The flowers I'd bought her on my way home were nestled between our bodies, the buds squished and bruised, as her grip on me tightened. For weeks, I'd felt like I was suffocating, but now, the sensation was welcomed. Hours seemed to pass as I held her close to me, enjoying the feeling of her body pressed against mine. I'd missed this. I'd missed *her*.

"I'm glad you're okay," she whispered against my chest.

"I'm so sorry, Jezebel. I had no idea it would escalate the way it did. Did she hurt you?"

I pulled her back to an arm's length from me so I could assess any damage. She shook her head. I reached for her, running my thumb along her jawline. She leaned into me, closing her eyes.

"I'm glad you're okay," I whispered, mimicking her words. "If she had hurt you..."

Angered, I pressed my lips together. My feelings for Abigail had changed. I no longer hated her, but I hated what she'd done. She knew of Jezebel's past. She may not have hurt Jezebel physically, but emotionally...

"It's okay, love. I'm fine. Come inside."

She pulled me through the threshold of our apartment

and locked the door. I waited for her to punch in the alarm code before she faced me.

"What happened?" she asked carefully.

I exhaled sharply. She needed to know. She *deserved* to know. But all I wanted to do was forget about it, move on, leave our demons in the past. Because it was finally over. I no longer needed to fear my past or the demons that lurked there. The pastor was gone. Abigail was gone. And the world had discovered my greatest secret, the existence of Living Light and the turmoil that surrounded a once peaceful place.

Instead, I said, "We should sit."

She nodded, and I walked to the couch, collapsing the moment I reached it. I glanced around. Jezebel had been cleaning the apartment—probably an attempt to keep herself busy while I dealt with the police. A moment later, she joined me on the couch and handed me a beer. She sipped on wine. I took a long chug before setting the bottle on the broken coffee table.

For a long time, while I gathered the words, we said nothing. She waited, patient with my attempt to unveil the horrors I'd been hiding.

"I'm ready now," I said softly.

She looked confused, so I elaborated.

"I'm ready to bare my truth," I said. "To you."

She swallowed and nodded. She never spoke. Instead, she waited for me to confess my sins.

"Abigail and I were engaged to be married."

Her eyes widened. "She wasn't lying? You two were *engaged?*"

I nodded. "It was a ploy, I'm sure, to win over the community. You see, my family controlled Living Light. My parents started it. From there, others joined. They became the unofficial leaders. When the pastor showed up, he wanted everything. He took control as leader, but many, including my parents, were against the idea of taking direction from a stranger. He thought joining Abigail and me would be like joining our two families. The idea did convince a lot of people to give him a chance at leadership."

"But you were young," she said.

I nodded. "I was. We both were. He didn't care. He used his daughter as a pawn. We didn't understand what it meant to be married, but we knew we didn't want that. We wanted to be kids."

"Understandable," she said, her tone short.

"It never would have been a real marriage. I'm still not convinced he was a real pastor. I think he just studied the Bible and used God's word when it was convenient for his goal."

She said nothing, so I continued.

"The day it... The day my parents and everyone else were murdered, I ran, like my mother told me to do. Hours later, I returned to find them all dead." I exhaled slowly, unable to look at Jezebel. "I just left them there. I ran into the surrounding woods and didn't stop until my legs gave out. Hikers found me. I wasn't too far from another town, so they brought me there, leaving me with the police. I never told anyone where I'd come from. They put me in foster care, and I left as soon as I could join the military."

She grabbed my hand, intertwining our fingers together. She traced hearts on my palm with her thumb. It was both erotic and empowering as I confessed my sins to her.

"I left them there to rot. My *own parents*. My friends. My community. I just left them behind, and I never looked back.

I never told anyone. I never gave them a proper burial or a second thought. I just pretended it never happened. At some point, the pastor returned, hid the evidence of Living Light, and sold the land. He buried my parents' bodies. It should have been me."

I was ashamed, embarrassed. Who does that? Who leaves their loved ones behind like food for the wild?

"For so many years, I felt dead inside—until I met you. You, with your unashamed brazenness, woke me. It was as if Abigail could sense my happiness, because right about that time, she came back into my life."

I felt Jezebel's grip tighten when I mentioned her captor's name.

"You should know I don't hate Abigail. Not anymore. Today, at the pastor's house..." I exhaled slowly, wondering how much I should confess. Did she want to know Abigail took her own life? Did she want to know how much of a monster the pastor truly was? I decided that I would not shield her from my past—even if that meant losing her. I needed to come clean, release my demons...forever.

"His name was Patrick Martin. I think, at one point, he loved his daughter. At least, I hope he did. I hope, even if it was brief, that he gave her a good life, because she dedicated hers to him, to his cause, without realizing how toxic he was. Because of him, she spent time in psychiatric hospitals. He sold my parents' land, their possessions, and stole everyone's money from Living Light, keeping it in overseas accounts."

"How... Did they tell you all of this today?"

I shook my head. "I hired a private investigator to track Abigail. Actually, I met him because of Abigail. I went through her coat pockets and found his card. He wouldn't tell me anything when I questioned him, quoting client-PI privilege, so I hired him."

She snorted, a wide smile crossing her face. "I'm not surprised. Did you tell the police?"

I nodded. "They know everything. I'm sure all that stolen money will sit in evidence somewhere. It should be donated to charity or go toward properly burying all his victims."

She smiled. "That would be nice. Maybe we can talk to someone about using the money to do something good."

I shrugged. I doubted the money would be handed over, but I appreciated the thought. "When we got to his apartment, he convinced her the only way we could be together was in death. So without hesitation, she killed herself. She just... She just believed in him so much that she took her own life."

"I'm so sorry, James. I'm so sorry you had to witness that," Jezebel said, leaning against me. She'd finished her wine and had set the empty glass right beside my half-empty beer bottle.

"He had to have known she was unstable. I just... I can't believe he'd speak to her that way. I can't believe he'd risk his daughter just to get rid of me. I feel...guilty. I was blinded by my rage. I didn't even know she was armed."

"Stop." She placed a finger against my lips and met my gaze. "Don't talk like that. What happened today was *not* your fault. What happened at Living Light was *not* your fault. Don't, even for a second, believe you could have changed what happened."

I smiled and placed a soft kiss on the pad of her finger. She ran it across my skin until it nestled in my hair. Straddling me, she pulled me into a deep kiss, and I welcomed every inch of her. I caressed her soft tongue with my own, relishing her flavor mixed with the wine she'd just finished. It was sweet yet tart. These were the moments I lived for, because I was able to release my pain and lose myself in Jezebel. We pulled away, breathless.

"How do you feel?" she asked me, running a hand through my hair.

"Dirty," I said.

She smiled. "Me too." Her eyes betrayed her arousal.

"I didn't mean in that way, but if you keep looking at me with your come-fuck-me eyes, I just might scratch that itch."

She laughed. "Why don't you take a quick shower and meet me on the roof?"

"You naughty minx," I said as I swatted her ass.

I stared at her, loving the way she looked at me. For so long, I'd feared my truth would scare her. I'd worried my lies would break what we had. I couldn't believe I'd doubted our love. What we had was true, real, raw, and once in a lifetime. No secret, no lie, no demons, could ever destroy what we shared.

"I love you, James."

"I love you, too. Always."

★ ★ ★

I found her on the rooftop deck, my skin still slick from my shower. I was grateful she'd offered me a brief reprieve rather than jumping into my pants, which was what she really craved.

The roof was our private domain. No one else in the building had access. After she'd moved in, she decorated it to her taste and included a sizable hot tub.

The sun had long since set, and the night was alive. The sounds of the city wafted up here, but they were dull, falling almost mute to my ears. As I walked toward her, the only lighting was from the moon, the stars, and the cityscape in the distance. For so long, I'd hated this city, but I could understand why Jezebel loved it so much. At night, with the building lights flickering in the distance, it was beautiful.

I found her soaking in the tub, her eyes closed. My body ached to join her and not just because I badly needed a relaxing soak. I dropped my towel and stepped into the hot water. It was scalding, but past experience assured me it wouldn't actually burn my flesh.

She opened her eyes as I sat down beside her. Turning, she rested her legs on my lap. I rubbed her feet, taking care to caress each toe, each heel, each tight calf. She moaned as I worked my way up her body. Over the past year, she'd slowly put on more weight, returning to her curvy frame. I cherished each deliciously soft curve.

I slid my hand between her legs, teasing her inner thigh. She moaned approvingly, biting her lower lip. My cock twitched in response.

She shimmied over to me, water splashing as she straddled my lap. She kissed me and ran her hands through my hair, tugging on the ends. She massaged my scalp as I stroked her tongue with my own. Sucking, nipping, licking, I poured my soul into this kiss.

She arched her back, rubbing my dick between her folds. She gasped into my mouth when I pressed her hard against me, rubbing her clit against my girth.

"Yes. Like that," she whispered, eyes closed as she leaned against me.

She lifted her ass until I slid inside her.

"Fuck," I said in a long, exaggerated moan. Between the heat of the water and the tightness of her pussy, I was sure I'd come too quickly.

She angled her hips and pumped herself on my dick. I sat back and watched. I kept my hands on her waist so I could feel her rise and fall as she took pleasure from me. She sank onto me over and over again, each time with more speed, more force. The water from the hot tub splashed onto the surrounding deck. I was absolutely positive there'd be no water left by the time we were finished, but I didn't care.

The hot tub's jets turned on, shooting water against my sore back. I leaned forward to give them better access and latched on to Jezebel's breast. I sucked her nipple, playfully nibbling the hard peak. When she cried out, I released it and licked away the pain.

"I'm going to come," she said.

Before I could respond, I felt her clench down on my dick. She screamed my name as she came, and I was sure our formerly blissfully unaware neighbors now knew exactly what we were doing up here. Maybe they should take lessons.

My orgasm followed soon after hers. She slowed and fell against me to catch her breath as I released myself inside her. She was limp in my arms, resting after a good fuck. Little did she know, I was nowhere near done with her.

I grabbed her ass, turned her over, and quickly sank back into her depths. My cock twitched. The lingering sensations of my recent orgasm still tickled. I pushed her forward to where I had been sitting, and she grasped the edge of the tub. I angled her hips as I slid in and out, slowly at first, buying time until the perfect moment.

"Fuck!" she yelled when the jets sprayed her. I was hoping I'd angled her body right, waiting for the moment the rush of constant water shot against her swollen clit.

I increased my speed, chasing another orgasm, and slammed into her, nearly sending her out of the hot tub. I sank my fingers into the flesh of her curvy hips.

"Don't stop, James," she said, breathless.

"Never," I promised.

EPILOGUE

I exhaled slowly as I assessed myself in the full-length mirror. My dress was tight. Was it too tight? My heels hurt. Would flats be acceptable? I heard the hallway floor creak as he approached. Taking one final glance, I scanned my body from head to toe. My hair was wrapped in a loose bun, flyaways untrappable, and I'd opted for simplistic makeup. Pressing my painted lips together, I smacked my mouth open and left the room.

"You look beautiful," James said.

I could feel my cheeks heat at his compliment. James always had a way of making me swoon, whether it was because of his words or his wicked-hot body.

"You don't look so bad yourself, handsome." I winked.

"Ready?" he asked.

I could tell he was nervous. This was his first time, and I remembered how nervous I was when I was in his situation.

I nodded. "Are *you* ready?"

"As ready as I'll ever be."

Hand in hand, we hailed a taxi, enjoying the ride in silence. Every time I glanced over, I wondered if I could find the words to strengthen him. Even going through a similar situation, I was unequipped to truly help him face his past. I opened my mouth to speak, only to snap it shut again.

We arrived twenty minutes later. My heels dug into the ground, and I cursed myself for not wearing flats. We made our way past others who, I was sure, were waiting for visitors as well. I prayed they wouldn't wait long.

When we reached them, I placed the flowers I'd been holding atop the soft, loose dirt.

"Hello, Mother. Father."

I wrapped my arm around James, pulling him close to me. I nuzzled into him, leaning my weight against him and anchoring him to this place. I thought he'd need that, to feel my weight, to feel held down here. I feared he'd float away, renouncing all emotion.

"I'm sorry... I'm sorry it's taken me as long as it has," he added.

I knew this was a big step for him, and I cherished the moment.

Their shared headstone was light gray with darker engraved lettering. It was simplistic and beautiful, like the two souls who once occupied the bodies buried beneath. They were long gone now, but I was sure they watched over him. Often, I told him how proud they'd be of him. He was an honorable man who had overcome a dark past. So many would have succumbed to the rage. It took a strong soul to emerge from the shadows, and I made sure he never forgot that.

We sat in silence until the sun began to set. Until I felt the tension within James lift. Until we both had, finally and truly, laid our demons to rest.

Keep reading for an excerpt!

EXCERPT FROM *NO PRINCE CHARMING*
BOOK ONE IN THE SECRETS OF STONE SERIES

Claire

April...

> *Oh my God.*
>
> The words sprinted through my head, over and over, as I prodded at my lips in assurance I wasn't dreaming. Or hopping dimensions. Or remembering the last half hour in a *really* crazy way. Or had hours passed, instead? I didn't know anymore. Time was suddenly contorted.
>
> *Oh. My. God.*
>
> What the hell had just happened?
>
> Forget my lips. My whole mouth felt like I'd just had dental work done, tingling in all the places his lips had touched moments ago—which had been everywhere.
>
> My mind raced, trying to match the erratic beat of my heart. "Christ," I whispered. My voice shook like a damn teenager's, so I repeated myself. Because *that* helped, right?
>
> Wrong. So wrong.
>
> It was all because of that man. That dictatorial, demanding...
>
> Nerve-numbing, bone-melting...
>
> *Man.*

Who really knew how to deliver a kiss.

Hell. That kiss.

Okay, by this age, I'd been kissed before. I'd been *everything* before. But after what we'd just done, I'd be awake for long hours tonight. *Long* hours. Shaking with need... Shivering with fear.

I pressed the Call button for the elevator with trembling fingers. Turning back to face the door I'd just emerged from, I reconsidered pushing the buzzer next to it instead. The black lacquer panel around the button was still smudged by the angry fingerprints I'd left when arriving here not more than thirty minutes ago—answering his damn summons.

Yeah. He'd summoned me. And, like a breathless backstage groupie, I'd dropped everything and come. Why? He was my hemlock. He could be nothing else.

I was even more pissed now. At him. At me. At the thoughts that wouldn't leave me alone now, all in answer to one tormenting question.

If Killian Stone kissed like that, what could he do to the rest of my body?

No. That kind of thinking was dangerous. The tiny hairs on the back of my neck stood up as if the air conditioner just kicked on at full power.

It had been a while since I'd been with a man. At least like...that.

Okay, it had been a long while.

For the last three years, career had come before all else. After the disaster I simply called the Nick Years, Dad had fought hard to help rebuild my spirit, including the doors he'd finagled open for me. Wasting those opportunities in favor of relationships wasn't an option. My focus had paid off, leading to a coveted position at Asher and Associates PR, where I'd quickly advanced to the elite field team for Andrea Asher herself. The six of us, including Andrea and her daughter, Margaux, were called corporate America's PR dream team. We were brought in when the blemishes were too big and horrid for in-house specialists, hired on a project-by-project basis for our thoroughness and objectivity. That also meant the assignments were intense, ruthless, and very temporary.

The gig at Stone Global was exactly such a job. And things were going well. Better than well. People were cooperating. The press was moving on to new prey. The job was actually ahead of schedule, and thank God for that. Soon, I'd be back in my rightful place at the home office in San Diego and what had just happened in Killian Stone's penthouse would remain no more than a blip in my memory. A very secret blip.

I shook my head in defiance. What was wrong with having lived a little? At twenty-six, I was due for at least one heart-stopping kiss with a man who looked like dark sin, was built like a navy SEAL, and kissed like a fantasy. *Sweet God, what a fantasy.*

"You didn't do anything wrong," I muttered. "You didn't break any rules...technically. He consented. And you sure as *hell* consented. So you're—"

Having an argument with yourself in the middle of a hallway in the Lincoln Park 2550 building, waiting on the world's slowest damn elevator.

I leaned on the Call button again.

While *still* trying to talk myself out of pouncing on Killian's buzzer too. Or perhaps back into it. If I could concoct an excuse to ring his doorbell before the elevator arrived...

No. This is dangerous, remember? He's dangerous. You

know all the sordid reasons why, his and yours.

Maybe I could just say I accidentally left my purse inside.

And that'll fly...how? One glance down at my oversize Michael Kors clutch had me cursing the fashion-trend gods, along with their penchant for large handbags.

I leaned against the wall, closing my eyes and hoping for a lightbulb. I was bombarded with Killian's smell instead. Armani Code. The cologne was still strong in my head, its rich bergamot and lemon mingling with the spice of his shampoo and the Scotch on his breath, like he'd scent-marked me through the intimacy of our skin...

My fingers roamed to my cheek, tracing the abrasion where he'd rubbed me with his stubble. My head fell back at the impact of the recollection.

In an instant, my mind conjured an image of him again, standing in front of me. Commanding. Looming. Hot...and hard. I felt his breath on my face again as he yanked me close. The press of his wool pants against my legs. The metallic scrape of his cufflinks on the wood of his desk as he shoved everything away to make room for our bodies. Then the wild throb of my heart as he tangled his hands in my hair, lifted my face toward his, and...

Yes.

The memory was so vivid, so good. I used the flat of my palm on my face now, thinking I could save the magic if I covered it. Protecting it from the outside world. Our perfect, shared moment in the middle of all this chaos.

Whoa.

"Get a grip." I dropped my hand along with the furious whisper. It was one kiss. Incredible, yes, but I guaranteed *he* wasn't still thinking about it like this. Behind that majestic door, Killian Stone moved again in his world, already focused on the next of his hundred priorities, none of them bearing my name. And he expected me to get back to mine, cushioning his company from that big, bad outside world I'd just been brooding over. *You've been hired to help clean up the Stone family's mess, not add to it.*

The elevator finally dinged.

At the same time, Killian's condo door opened behind me.

I locked a smile on my face, trying to look like I had been patiently waiting for the elevator the entire time.

"Miss Montgomery?"

Not Killian. I didn't know whether to curse or laugh.

"Yes?" I managed a Girl Scout-sweet reply.

A kind face was waiting when I turned around. The man wore such a warm expression I was tempted to call him Fred. *Not* Alfred. Just Fred. The man was too handsome for a full Alfred.

Fred handed me a small ivory envelope and then stepped over into the elevator. He held the doors open while I got into the car with him. We rode in silence down to the lobby. I squirmed while Fred smiled as if it were Saturday in the park. Did he know what his boss had just done with me?

I winced toward the wall. Technically, Killian was *my* boss right now too.

Mr. Stone. Mr. Stone. Mr. Stone.

He can never be "Killian" again.

The sooner you remember that, the better.

I was dying to open that little envelope but carefully slipped it into my queen-size clutch for when I was alone again in the cab on my way back to the hotel.

"I'll call the car round for you." Like his employer, Fred

made it obvious the subject wasn't up for debate, so I forced a smile and followed him across the gleaming lobby to the building's front awning. In less than a minute, the black town car with the Stone Global logo on its doors appeared. I climbed in, all the while yearning for the anonymity of a city cab instead.

Chicago was a great city, but the traffic was insane, even as evening officially blended into nighttime. Nevertheless, Killian's building was swiftly swallowed by the lush trees of the neighborhood. I was on my way back to the hotel. Back to real life—and all the dangers that waited if anyone on the team ever learned where I'd just been.

For just a few more seconds, I yearned to remember the fantasy instead. Perhaps the treasure in my purse would help.

I pulled it out, running reverent fingers over it again. Nothing was written on the outside. Killian—Mr. Stone—had simply expected it would be delivered straight to me.

The elegant handwriting inside, dedicated to just one sentence, dried out my throat upon impact.

I must see you again.

**This story continues in book one of the
Secrets of Stone Series: No Prince Charming!**

ALSO BY DANIELLE ROSE

Pieces of Me Duet:

Lies We Keep

Truth We Bear

**For a full list of Danielle's other titles,
visit her at DRoseAuthor.com**

ACKNOWLEDGMENTS

This book wouldn't be published without the amazing team at Waterhouse Press: Meredith, Jon, Scott, Robyn, Haley, and the many minds behind proofreading, formatting, and marketing. I wouldn't be where I am in my career without your expertise. Words could never express how grateful I am to have met you all.

To Heather—you hold a special place in my heart, and it is fair to say this book is as good as it is because of your guidance. Thank you for all you've done.

To my readers—I love you all. Every day, I get to do what I love to do because you read my books. Thank you for giving me a chance.

And finally, to those bearing the pain of love lost—this one is for you. Find truth. Find hope. Find happiness... Again.

ABOUT DANIELLE ROSE

Dubbed a "triple threat" by readers, Danielle Rose dabbles in many genres, including urban fantasy, suspense, and romance. The *USA Today* bestselling author holds a Master of Fine Arts in creative writing from the University of Southern Maine.

Danielle is a self-professed sufferer of 'philes and an Oxford comma enthusiast. She prefers solitude to crowds, animals to people, four seasons to hellfire, Nature to cities, and traveling as often as she breathes.

Visit her at DRoseAuthor.com